When The Blood Runs Warm

—❧—

Sugar

From the Author

G od! YOU DID THAT THANG!!! I am so grateful to you for everything you do. Our talks mean the world to me. I owe you me and I strive daily to make you happy.

Gal! Thank you. We've come a long way, but the journey has been just as satisfying as the destination. I'm learning to peel the onion and I will continue to learn how to take care of Shalonda. Thank you for understanding and teaching me how to be patient with myself.

Daryl, you're still here! The heart attack was rough. You pulled through better than anyone expected and I'm glad you did. I enjoy our movie dates and conversations. I'm so glad you're living and loving it.

My support system; Koree, Michael, Aunt Linnie, Uncle Don, the whole gang (you know who you are). I don't even know where to start. Thank you, all of you.

To Second Street Bean and Half Shell Oyster House (Hattiesburg location), thank you. You were a mini vacation when I needed to rest my mind and fill my belly. I used you as a reset for my creative juices and it worked every single time. Your atmospheres are amazing.

To friends and enemies. Thank you for everything! I am the best version of me because of you.

To you, the reader. I wrote this book because I needed a friend. I needed someone to lean on during a very difficult time. I hope this book brings you the laughter and enjoyment it brought me. This story gave me hope. I pray it gives you the same.

Read. Grow. Love.

Sugar

Chapter

1

<u>Dahlia Daceion Emerley</u>

"I just don't think it's a good idea. You know I love you and all Dee. I just don't want to become a hot topic. I mean, what will the people at church say? You know that's the most influential people in this town. They work at banks, hospitals and police stations. They can make us all outcasts. We grew up with these people Dee. I want you to be happy, but not at such an expense. I mean...people talk. People gone be talking about us and not just you. They gone think we are all funny just 'cause we hang with you. Why you gotta bring the chick to church? Why can't we have a gathering and invite certain people over for your coming out event?"

This girl gets on my very last nerves; especially when she takes a subject about anybody else and turns it into her own one woman play. Liberty Patrice Talbert is not just one of my best friends, she is like my sister. We hardly ever agree on anything but food and our love for each other.

"Oh so that's how we rolling now? You being seen as 'funny' is your biggest concern Liberty? Hmm? Ms. My-boyfriend's-wife-just-keyed-my-car! And by the way, I was there for that and all the other sinful things you seemed to get yourself into. Don't sit here and act like you and Jesus graduated from high school together. Of all the times I've been there for you, why is it so hard for you to be here for me? Damn it Lib! It's one church service. ONE! This is Columbia Mississippi. You know damn well that if you bring your significant other to church you're making a statement. So only straight people get to make that statement? And believe you me, everybody in that church knows you are straight. Trust me, they latch on to their husbands when you 'Enter His gates with thanksgiving', okay?"

Well, she didn't like that. That shut her right up. I don't like hurting the girl's feelings, but I swear she knows how to rub me the wrong way. Looking at her face drop to the top of her stomach gave me very little satisfaction. Now I hate that I've said it. Lib's getting to the point where I'm not comfortable being me around her and we've been friends way too long for that. But we gone have to schedule that convo for a later date and a more private setting where she'll feel comfortable enough to open up and tell it all. She tends to keep secrets from the rest of the group. For the life of me, I don't know why.

"Now Dahlia, you didn't have to do the girl like that!" Chevy stopped for a good old country laugh. It calmed my anger down a bit. You can always count on Chevy for that. "Liberty. My sweet, dramatic, self-centered Liberty; Dee ain't told you nothing but the truth. Stop acting like you right when everybody that has ever spent more than an hour with you knows that you ain't. Neither am I. But we all have been there for you and all your wrong doing. We ain't never judged you on any of it. I even fought a married woman because of one of your entanglements with her husband. Stop acting like you on the straight and narrow. 'Cause both the seeing and the blind know you ain't. Now I will say this. If you are comfortable enough in your own skin Dee, bring your girlfriend to church. Let 'em talk. They talkin 'bout cho funny ass anyway, I can guarantee it. Your messy and hateful mama making sure of it. So I say give 'em a good n hot topic. Show them lying biddies you happy and you ain't ashamed."

Talking while she's rolling her neck and snapping her fingers. That's my girl Chevy. She's a little tipsy. Lately she's always a little tipsy. She's been headed toward drunkard drive ever since she lost her husband around six months ago. We deal with it because we don't know how to address it. What do you tell a woman you've known all your life about losing what we all knew to be the love of her life? Especially when we are all too inexperienced to know what "in love" is. A very few people know her real name. Shevelle Marie Davidson. However, she's been Chevy since she was brought home from the hospital. They didn't even call her government name at graduation.

"Byrd, why are you so quiet? Everyone has said their peace except for you. Gone and let me hear it." Kamdyn Korede' Byrd is the sweetest, most thoughtful, easy going 21 year old you'll ever meet. She's the baby of the group.

We all feel the need to "take care" of her. We all pitched in and bought her a car for graduation so she could travel back and forth to school. We also took her to the health department for her first Depo shot. She was going to be somebody, without babies. We all were going to help make sure of that. Thankfully she's studying to be a lawyer. We need someone in the bunch with some knowledge to get me out of trouble. I always talk to her at the end of the day because she's got such a soothing voice and such a calm spirit. Now don't get me wrong, when she's mad she'll make you feel like she can set the whole world on fire, light a cigarette and watch it burn. She's cool headed, til she's not. She's just the perfect person to put me in my place.

"Dahlia, I agree with Chevy and Liberty. I feel like you know what you're gonna get yourself into. It's gonna get good, bad and ugly. No matter what, you've got my support and I'll happily cuss out them old biddies on your behalf. But know, it's going to be an epic mess."

She was right. Maybe I didn't put enough thought into my decision of stepping out in public. I mean, I ain't never been shy about my sexuality. But I ain't never just put my business out there either. And I really didn't think about how it would affect the girls. When Byrd said she'd fight for me, it made me realize that I'm not in this alone. I don't mean to be selfish. It's just I didn't want to think about what I do affecting other people. People don't seem to think about me when they make decisions.

"Alright. Y'all done put plenty on my brain for me to consider. I'll think about it some more. I really don't wanna cause any trouble for y'all. And with that, I'm out. I gotta work tonight." I said my goodbyes and ended our weekly video chat. We keep in touch. We text one another every day. But it's not enough. We're a family and we are used to seeing each other every day because we lived down the same drive. We'd got so used to seeing each other's face that when we don't, we feel like something just ain't right. And for strange reasons unknown, I got that exact feeling right now.

Something is off with Liberty; I can see it in her eyes. I saw that "One flew over the Cuckoo's Nest" look on her face. She's one of those people who is needy; constantly in search of love whether it's in the wrong places or the right ones. She and I have a connection that she shares with no one else. When her mother gave her away to her aunt, I was right there. When she came back two years later badly beaten, I was right there. And when she left once again without her daughter, I was right there. While her mother was dying with AIDS, I was right there. And when her father tried to forcefully take her away from her house because he wanted to claim her as his own personal slave, I was right there with a gun. Liberty is my sister and my responsibility. Because of my love and history with her, I'll table my feelings for now 'cause I have to make sure she's really okay.

"Baby? You got that look in your eyes. You okay?" Na'Treiel "Tracey" James entered my living room and my brain storm. This smooth talking, honey brown eyed, silky dark-skinned, yet rough edged chick of mine has developed the habit of reading me like a book. I tried to mask my concern for Liberty with a carefree, "Hey!" She answered with a kiss to the cheek. "Don't play me. Whatever is on your mind, just know that I'm down." This is why I wanna take her to church with me. I mean ain't nobody been able to make me feel empowered like this. Not even my girls. I need to show her that I appreciate her and she means so much to me. "You don't even know what I'm thinking about. How you just gone endorse it like that?" She gave me that look. You know what look I'm talking about. The one that says 'girl please'. I just shook my head and giggled. I knew I was caught. I may as well go ahead, open my mouth and allow the thoughts to fly out.

"Something is up with Liberty. I need to find out what it is and help fix it. The way her eyes were looking, it's just the beginning of the issue. I need to nip it in the bud before it's too late. Unfortunately, I don't have the time. I need to be at the hospital in 7 hours. That's just enough time to eat, shower, and sleep. And I won't be able to get off til Saturday morning." I pause. That ain't like me to pause in the middle of the thought flow. I need to spend some time alone and figure out what's going on with me. I have been doing some changing in spite of myself. I am doing too much thinking around Tracie. I'm considering her feelings entirely too much. I don't like that.

"Which reminds me, I'm not ready for us to make an appearance as a couple at church. Is that alright?" I rubbed her arm and watched her face for some type of sign of disappointment. When she sighed as if she was relieved and smiled, I began to wonder if I was being selfish. Was I pushing for something that she didn't even want? She spoke the words that forever changed me. "I just want you. I don't care about what anybody else wants. I ain't studdin' what they think. As long as you are happy when you think about us, no one has to know and everybody can know. It's just me and you sugar." I hugged her and cried. We've only been together a few months. She's shown me that I could rely on her to simply love me. Everybody relies on me to be there for them. To be the strong one, to be the wise one. Family, friends,and co-workers are all the same. "What can you do for me, Dahlia?" That's the question everybody seems to ask, even if it is down the road in the relationship. Tracie hasn't asked for the keys to my car, no money, hasn't even asked for the key to my house. Just wanted my heart. That's why I love her so much.

So I'll cancel the show-n-tell appearance at church. It was childish of me anyway, I guess. I pulled away from her and wiped my eyes. She held my face in her strong, soft hands and kissed me tenderly; completely. It wasn't one of those passionate "do me" kisses. It was a kiss that speaks to the soul. When she let go of me I felt completely different. I was totally relaxed, sleepy even. I couldn't seem to feel my feet on the ground, or the weight of my shoulders. And for the strangest reason I couldn't stop staring at her lips. They were glossy, peach and inviting. It was like her lips had me mesmerized. "Tracie?" I didn't recognize my own voice. I sounded drunk and far away. She still had her eyes closed soaking in the moment. "What did you do to me?" Her eyes fluttered open and she smiled. "What do you mean, my love?" I tried to look at her in a mischievous fashion. It didn't work. She laughed, very softly, and said; "Don't try it baby. I've got you under my skin. Deep in the heart of me."

She hummed the rest of the old song I loved so much. I smiled and laid back on the sofa bed I've come accustomed to sleeping on because I need a new mattress. She laid beside me watching me and stroking my arm as I dozed off to sleep. That was so perfect. The touch felt against my skin. The wind of her breath floating across me. It was like a spring day. I will never be able to understand the vibes I felt in that moment. Something in the back of my head told me that something ain't quite right. I've been feeling that tugging, nagging, dread of an intuition for about a month now. But today, just like yesterday, I'll happily ignore it again as I drift off to sleep.

Chapter

2

<u>Liberty Patrice Talbert</u>

She ain't have to put me all the way out there! I know everybody else knew it but, still! I swear Dahlia loves throwing me under the bus to make herself look better. When she knows good and well her mess stinks worse than mine! At least my wrong is natural. But on one hand, Tracie makes her happier than I've ever seen her. And she deserves to be happy. She's been through so much. Because of me alone she's seen the inside of a jail cell. And has seen it more than once. She has always been there for me. I may not be able to do for her what she's done for me. I know I can't. At least I can be happy for her happiness. It's just that Auntie Beatrice raised me deep off in the church. I just can't support two women joining together!

"Get out your thoughts and cook me some breakfast girl! You done lost your damn mind not having me something to eat when I wake up. That's why I can't leave my wife for you. You gone have to grow the hell up and take care of your man. Not be on the phone with them silly heifers you call friends." I honestly forgot about what time it was. I usually have his food ready. Hold up. I'm tripping. Did he just down talk my girls? "Uh...look, don't go there. I know you didn't just dis my friends. That's one line you don't cross. Matter of fact you can get your stuff and go right on back to 'yo wife' and stay your cheating, trifling, low-down, hungry ass right there."

Shoot! I ain't mean to say that! I don't know what got into me. When Jeffery Omar Daley and I met, it was an instant attraction. He's a sexy 6'2 red boned man with just enough muscles to hold you down. He has a gold tooth in the front, and a smile that could light up a room. He also has a country laugh that's contagious. I didn't want him to go, but it will be a snowstorm in hell before I let him come between me and my family, be it blood or not. I got up and started packing his clothes for him. He was still dressed in a wife-beater and boxers. I didn't care. Ain't nobody gonna disrespect me. The loving ain't that good. He finishes too quickly anyway. Plus he couldn't cook. I got to have a man who can at least cook. The way I see it, God made a decision for me. I just went with it. It was time for brother-man to go.

Before I knew what happened, he grabbed me, swung me hard into the wall, and slapped the taste out of my mouth. I fell to the floor. "So you have lost your mind. Don't you ever talk to me like that. You do what I tell you to do, when I tell you to do it. You belong to me. I'm your daddy, you crazy hoe. You get your lazy ass up off that floor and make my breakfast before I make you regret the day you were born. You hear me?!"

Wrong thing to do. And even worse things to say. I came up with my Glock 43. I'm 5'3, slender, cute and shy. You'd never think in a million years that I'm military with specialty training in weapons and close quarters combat. I became numb. My breathing was no longer labored, it was even and smooth. My voice became dark, deep, and deadly. "Say it again. I dare you. I belong to me. Nobody owns me, never will." I watched the fear of God quickly enter into his eyes. He stood there with his hands up, silent. "I'm going to say this again. Get your shit and step your rusty heels out of my house." He had a plea in his eyes. I no longer cared for him. I saw the features of my father in his face. Once that happens, the infatuation is over and the trouble begins. As he started to pack, I'd point to things he was forgetting with the gun.

"Come on baby, I didn't mean to. You just seem to take me there sometimes. I have feelings for you baby. Don't end it like this. We can have something special." Oh he was just a lying. I paid his lips no attention. Everything was going in one ear and out the other. I was watching him with my gun still aimed at his head. He got everything and headed to the door. "Jeffery, my key." He threw it on the counter with some funk on it. "An attitude? Make sure you leave all the money in your wallet on the counter too. I'll deduct it from the loan of 5,000 you borrowed from me. And I collect with interest." He emptied out his wallet. Slammed the money on the counter, mumbled under his breath, and slammed my door. I didn't hear what he said. But me being the girl I am, I've got to have the last word. I stepped out of my front door, and shot his car up before he could get in it. He was on the ground hollering like the punk he is.

I walked back in the house and closed my door and chuckled to myself. Nobody hits me and gets away with it. "Silly heifers my ass," I said aloud to myself. Nobody talks about my girls in my face and doesn't get the fear of God put in them. I walked around the house making sure he didn't leave anything. If he did, I'd have a burning ceremony in my back yard. I feel like I need to purge my home and my life of this foolish Negro. My soul needs purging. I need to repent to God for the mess I made with my eyes wide open. It's not like I didn't know he was married. I met his wife when I met him. But when he approached me, I couldn't say no. "Okay God. I'm sorry I didn't crucify the flesh. I know it was wrong but I did it anyway. Help me to make better decisions. Help me Lord." I knew I had to do better. I can't lead anyone towards God out here acting like "hoe is life". That's the last married man, I swear it. "I'm sorry God. I am." Right before I was about to turn my music on and clean my house, I heard sirens in the distance. "Well let me play my part", I said to no one in particular. See I have a very honest face. Plus, I'm yellow-boned and easily bruised. I can be the victim easily. He doesn't have a scratch on him. The tears on my face were for God...but the officers don't have to know everything, right?

"BAM! BAM! BAM!" I walk to the door and open it partly. I only show half of my face, the part that's fine of course. The hurt side is shown last for dramatic effect. "Yes?" I tried to sound half strong, half tired which wasn't hard to do since it's the truth. The sight that awaited me at my front door was absolute beauty. "Ma'am, I'm Officer Calloway with the Marion County Sheriff's department and we are here because this man called us thinking his life was in danger. And judging by the holes in his car, we're inclined to believe him. Can you step out on the front porch for me?" I couldn't help but notice how handsome this man was. Let me run it down for you. 5 '10, caramel, bulging muscles under the uniform, straight pearly whites, one deep dimple in each cheek, two small beauty marks on his left eyelid, and a voice as smooth and rough as Ving Rhames'. I need some prayer because between the way he looks and the thoughts that are running through my mind, my headlights were on bright. Ooh Liberty, get it together. You're a professional. Breathe smooth and even, not hot and heavy.

"Yes sir. Let me go get a more suitable shirt." It's time to turn up the heat and be the sweet yet tired battered little girlfriend. "By the way, here's the gun." I opened the door wider to show the bruises and handed it to him in a defenseless fashion, handle first. He smiled and good God Almighty! The warmth of him spread all over me. Then his face turned serious as he saw my whole face and he said, "Whoa, look at that shiner." He grabbed my shoulder gently. I shuddered at his touch. "Is that a bruise on your arm?" I just nodded. He said, "If you can, put on a short-sleeved or sleeveless shirt and shoes. Grab your purse and keys, I'm going to take you to the station for pictures." I nodded again with more tears in my eyes. That wasn't an act. There was a kindness in this man: his voice, eyes and touch; that I've never seen in any man before. I was taken aback. I mentally made it my mission to either get next to this officer or not settle for anything less than a man with his spirit.

I left the door open while I walked back to my room to get a spaghetti strapped shirt and flip flops. I could hear men mumbling. My wallet/phone duo and keys were right there by the door. When I stepped outside again, locking the door behind me, I saw Jeffery in the back of a squad car. If looks could kill, I'd have dropped dead on my front porch amongst all of these witnesses. It looked like he'd try revenge later on. I made another mental note to change all the locks and the passcodes to all my accounts, especially the security codes to the house ASAP.

"Okay, are you ready? Not just for the ride, but to press charges?" Officer Good looking Calloway said. He was straight to the point. So, I guess I will be too. Because truth be told, I was excited to let the cat out the bag. I wanted his wife to know that he was at my house being put in his place. I will never allow a man to beat me. And if she was getting hit, it was because she was weak. And I ain't weak baby. "Yeah, I'm ready. Question is, are you ready for the whole story?" He just smiled at me sympathetically and nodded in the affirmative.

Chapter

3

<u>Shevelle Marie Davidson</u>

Tweet was singing her heart out. She was telling the absolute truth. "I fell for the small talk, and you made me believe…I got whatcha want, I'm whatcha need." I was just a singing along to Ms. Charlene, driving fast with the windows down. That wind in my ears did more than drown out my off key harmonizing skills. It sobered me. Made me feel again. Something I've been trying to avoid for months. Since I'm driving, I'm not going to drink. I do follow the instructions on the bottle. I drink responsibly. Unfortunately, I shouldn't have had that liquid courage in the cute flute at the restaurant. Then I wouldn't be driving home at three in the morning. Oh he was 100 percent fine and a smooth talking brother to the hilt. But by the time I realized who he was, it was too late. Evan Lamont Richardson Jr., my eighth grade crush.

He's a lawyer now. But when I thought he was the "man", he was trying to take the presidential seat of the student council. He was tall and lanky. Brown skinned and long eyelashes. Big smile with a mouth full of braces. His skin was smooth and his cheekbones were high. That's why most girls like him. But what remembered most about him was those eyes; big, brown and puppy dog. I don't think he even knew my name. Time passed and we graduated together. Him and all of his honors and scholarships and of course, that presidential seat in the student body; I'd lost interest. He was still cute with those big brown eyes. But I had my heart snatched from my chest by the basketball star of the class before me. It's been twelve years since our graduation night. Honestly I'd forgotten all about Evan.

For some odd reason, my co-workers wanted to meet up and have a night of fun. The odd part was I joined them. I usually drink at home or with my crew. But I wanted to do something a little different. So we met up at this really fancy bar and grill type of place. The food was good. The drinks were social. And the company was so-so. But that live music was intoxicating with every beat. Between that coconut-flavored flute and that sound, I was on cloud 9. My burnt orange high-low spaghetti strapped dress was fitting this dark chocolate size 8 like a dream. I had pulled my gay co-worker to the floor and I had a blast. He was getting it on in there. He was teaching me new dances, rocking in sync with me on the old moves.

We were having strange eyes roam the both of us. He whispered in my ear, "If I were straight, I'd be very jealous of those dark brown sad eyes staring at you from the bar. Work it honey! You might get to go see somebody else's bedroom tonight." I laughed and put my arms around his neck. He swung me around for a great view of the bar. And good God Almighty! There he was. Tall, brown, and built; looking like a commercial for a gym and an orthodontist all rolled up into a 6'1 frame. He was looking like a meal but I had to treat him like a snack. You never lay all your cards on the table. No matter what the situation or the emotion. You keep some things to yourself until it feels right. Hey, timing is everything. But so is truth.

When the song was over, I told Jasper that his next drink was on me. As a thank you for showing me such a good time. He replied, "Thank ya honey! Now go on and get that phone number from that good looking man." I swear, every woman needs a gay guy as a friend. They make you feel like a real woman. I just smiled and turned around to do just what he said. I smoothed my dress down with my hands and strutted to the bar like my name was Blanche Devereaux. The click-click of my heels gave me some sho nuff confidence. It made me feel sexy and sure of myself. And some of that could be contributed to that second flute of midnight kiss. As I got to the bar, right next to him I might add, I ordered Jasper's Blue Hawaii and my last midnight kiss of the night. "You are some kind of hot out there on that dance floor, young lady." The bartender said. He was older, but handsome. You could tell he had daughters my age because his eyes didn't roam. And he had a protective quality to his voice. "Thank you sir. I needed to 'hang my 9-5 up on the shelf' I guess." He smiled and nodded as if to reply that he knew exactly what I meant.

"Chevy. You haven't aged a day over 17. You are absolutely beautiful." I turned around to look that handsome man in his face with the biggest question mark etched in mine. "How have you been?" I wasn't going to let on that I had no earthly idea who he was. "Life has treated me well. I have no complaints." I was my smart mouthed self as usual. But I added a little spice to it. I let my eyes do some wandering from his head to his shoes.

"That I can see." It was then that he flashed that 2 million dollar smile. I knew exactly who he was. "It's been quite a long time. What blew you this way Evan?" He was impressed. He had a smirk and a nod. "My mother had hip surgery this past Wednesday. So I came home to help my sister. If I hadn't I'd have never heard the end of it." Hmm...I didn't know his mom. That's a shame. I could kiss her cheek for producing the vision of beauty standing before me. "So, you've been being the good son?" He nodded as he sipped his drink. By the look and the smell, it was an old fashioned. Hey...I know my liquor.

"Well let me help you work off a little stress. Follow me." He looked at me from the side of his eye. I figured he thought I was crazy. But he followed. Good boy! I carried the drinks to the middle of the dance floor. And as if he was reading my thoughts, Jasper met me to take the drinks from my hands. He didn't say a word. He just winked. At that moment two things happened. One, I made a mental note to get Jasper a Christmas present. Two, I took control. The second one took me by surprise. I've been allowing liquor to control most of my actions for the last four months. I think it's time to stop.

As I felt hands grab my hips, I decided I was going to leave all my troubles on the dance floor, including my obsessive drinking. I gave the place a show. I gave it all I had. I'm doing all the dances I remembered plus the new ones I was taught. I'm flirting and encouraging Evan; who is giving me a run for my money. I'm having the time of my life.

When I realized I'm out of breath and not as young as I once was, I decided to call it a night. I paid the waitress. She glanced in Evan's direction and said, "Looks like you're leaving with way more than you came with. Have a wonderful night ma'am." I just smiled and nodded. Honestly because I was too breathless to say much. With every step he took towards me, the brain was telling me to run away. But his smile paralyzed me. I couldn't move. "Chevy, come spend a little time with me tonight?" His words freed me. I was able to speak and move after he spoke. "I'd love to. Coffee sounds good to me. You?" He nodded and extended his hand to me.

The heat from his hand reached me; past my desires and right into my heart. Truth be told, I want him sexually and emotionally. The sex, is normal. I'm not bugging off that. But my emotions have been all over the place. They can't be trusted. Which is why I drink so heavily. But if I'm going to slow up on the bottle, I'm going to have to face these emotions head on.

"Your place or mine?" He asked so smoothly I got confused. I guess he thought I was drunk because it took me so long to answer. "Just follow me Chevy", once he got me to my truck. I did as I was told. While I was driving, I gave myself a pep talk. "Shevelle Marie! Ooh honey he is so fine. And those teeth tell you he gots money. I had so much fun with him. But do I want him tonight? I mean yeah I know him and all but you don't let 'em hit on the first night. What am I talking about? I've had many and plenty of hitter quitters in the last three months. Do I want something more from this?" I was driving myself crazier than I already was. But if I just go with it, I won't be able to look him in the eye in the morning.

His car stopped. He'd led me to the hotel where he was staying. I parked, sprayed perfume in all the right places, and got out of the Tahoe. It was then when I realized I was in my husband's truck. I looked down at my hands and saw my wedding ring. I was reminded that I was still some man's wife. It didn't matter that he was dead. He was still my life partner. And until I dealt with it, he still owned me.

Evan walked over to the truck, grabbed my hand and led me to the door, through the lobby, up the stairs, down the hall and to his room without saying one word. He reached in his back pocket and pulled out his key card, opened the door and led me inside. His suite was fancy, roomy and clean. I sat in a chair while he closed the door and took off his shoes. He grabbed my hands, stood me up and slid his hands on both sides of my face. He kissed me. Now when I say he kissed me, I mean he made my knees weak and my breaths quick. He made my eyes close and my palms sweat. This man kissed the weary woman out of my soul and the innocent eighth grade girl back into it. It scared me to death!

I haven't had that happen to me...EVER! This man right here was gone make me go all in. My mind said "RUN!!" But my feet said, "Stay". He pulled me close to him and wrapped his arms around me. I could feel his chest and arms. I could tell he was excited by the bulge but his actions were slow and methodical. It was like he was pacing this thing out. Like he had a schedule and he had no intention of rushing it. His mouth traveled down to my collar bone and his hands down and laced together just under my bottom. That's when I lost strength in my legs. He just held me up like he expected for it to happen. That's when he broke the kiss and eased me down on top of the table. He didn't lay me down, he sat me down.

After a whole lot of heavy breathing, he eased his hands up my arms and asked, "Chevy. How have you been holding up?" Now why he gotta with the questions!? I'm enjoying being 14 and fast right now. Here he decides to make me 30 and broken again. He needs to figure out which "Chevy" he wants to make me! Got my emotions and mindset running wild with that kissing! Lawd that KISS!! Let me pace my breathing before he has to hand me a brown paper bag. "What do you mean?" He smiled at me. "I kissed you with desire and passion to see how you'd respond. Your reaction would tell me what your words wouldn't; how you are really doing." I just stared at him with a blank face. I didn't know what to say. "By that kiss alone, I know that you've been having a rough time. I'm not going to take advantage of that. Instead I'm going to make you coffee like you asked. And I'd love it if you stayed the night with me. If only to talk."

Honestly, my body was pissed! I mean, from one kiss he had the headlights on bright, the panties wet, and the breathing labored. I just knew this was going to be the one night stand by which all others would be judged. However my mind began to settle, which made the nervousness calm down. I could only nod my head yes because I didn't trust my words. There was too much going on inside of me. "If you'll allow, this is the first of many nights of coffee we'll have together." Evan smiled and had some sexy confidence that made the smart mouthed 30 year old take control again.

Chapter

4

<u>Kamdyn Korede' Byrd</u>

I am doing the best I can to follow along with the professor with the hum-drum voice. It's not quite as bad as the "Clear Eyes" commercial commentator, but it ain't far from it. I purposefully leave my phone in the car so that I don't distract myself from class. But man I need a distraction! Besides political science ain't really on my mind. I'm preoccupied with the words that this fine brother said last night at the bar. "You'll get what you want, but it won't be enough to keep you satisfied." What in the world did he mean? Why is it still ringing loud in my head? And why do I feel like crying when I think about it? Is it possible to work hard and achieve and be empty?

Yeah yeah, I know all about the Sunday School Version of the story but I'm a grown woman doing the best I can to succeed and survive. I put God first, six days outta seven. I keep my nose clean and my money safe. What else am I supposed to do? "Hey...you got notes?" Says the boy that sits beside me in just about every class I have. He thinks I'm his school-house girlfriend or something. I simply just looked at him and shook my head. He looked at me disappointed. He had no idea how much I didn't care. I turned my attention back to Professor Hum-drum.

After class was over, Shawn caught up to me. "Kay, what's going on with you? We are Starksy and Hutch. We work well together. You haven't been on your game. You need to come on with it." I am so tired of carrying this dude on my shoulders. The buck stops...right here and right damn now. "Wait. Wait. Wait a minute. Starksy and Hutch were partners. They had each other's back.

Not one mooching off the other. Tell me one thing you have done for me since we've met?" He looked so hurt. I didn't feel he had the right to be.

"I'm waiting Shawn. Spit it out." I crossed my arms, leaned back and tapped my foot waiting for a response. His mouth was moving but no sound came out. I rolled my eyes and started to walk away. He grabbed my arm and swung me around. "Baby please, I'm not going to be able to pass this class without you." Jesus, leeches have legs! "This class?" I shook his hand off my arm. "Boy you can't pass ANY class without me. And I ain't-cha baby. I don't find you remotely attractive. You're not in high school anymore dude. You gotta work to get it, not copy off me. Think fool! How is it you copy off me and make C's and I make straight A's? I put in the work. I don't have to listen to the lectures and take notes. I read the books before I even take the courses. I get as much pre-education as I can before I step foot in classes. I volunteer at the courthouses and law offices to get as much experience and knowledge as possible. I put in the work bruh! I need to come on with it? You need to leave it alone."

I'd had enough. How is it that I can maintain a 4.0 GPA and a full time job and this man-child can't even take adequate notes? I'm not in the mood. He better tuck his tail between his legs and go on somewhere. I turn to walk off. "Kay? Please." I just kept walking. I was hoping he wasn't following me. 'Cause he was gone taste this piece. I trust nobody if you ain't family, by blood or love. Life has taught me that lesson the hard way. I have been hurt and taken advantage of for a long time. Life is a beast and it can make you into a monster. When I glanced over my shoulder, I realized that I wasn't being followed. I breathed a sigh of relief because I didn't want to hurt Shawn any more than I already have. A wounded ego takes a long time to heal, but blunt force trauma to the head will land me in jail.

I get in my car and head to the Shell Station back home. Only in the south can you get a good, home cooked, full three course meal at a gas station. I think the same people who cook at the church on big meeting Sunday cook at the Shell "Coop De Ville" Monday through Friday. Now on Saturday the deacons must barbeque. That is the very best I've ever had. They got to be humming those old spirituals while they smoked that meat.

I've got about two hours before I get home so I may as well do what I always do; talk my feelings out. Nobody hears me but God. Somehow in those two hours more sense is made than a whole weeks' worth of lectures and studying. I have been talking to God so much lately. I've been paying attention to my surroundings and I've been seeing His response to our conversations. It's been mind blowing. "Okay God. Let's talk." I even make sure my passenger seat is clean and empty so He feels welcomed. "So, I wanna know if you sent that good looking man to the bar last night to talk to me. And if you did, can I keep him?" I had to laugh at my own self.

"For real though God, He was some kind of fine. The thing that stuck out the most was his ability to have a conversation. That's like seeing a snow white lion in the desert. It's impossible!" I take a minute to sip on tea and not look absolutely crazy at the red light. I mean, I'm not ashamed of God. But I don't want to go to the nut house either. Once the light turned green, I resumed our conversation. "Lord, that fine specimen of a man said something to me that sounded like you. And that scared the daylights out of me. 'You'll get what you want, but it won't be enough to keep you satisfied', now what does that mean? I am doing the best I can to make it to where I depend on nobody but you. Starting out as a bartender was a smart move as far as becoming independent. It allowed me to live comfortably and the hours worked so well with my school schedule. I am happy with all my choices. I have no regrets. But what he said at the bar got me second guessing everything. God, show me what it is that I need to know. Make me see what I'm missing." I stopped talking and started thinking. 'What if' is a powerful tool of chaos. I want to be and remain clear headed. I've always been the voice of reason for my crew. I can't allow words that yet have meaning to interrupt that. I'm going to have to throw all of the "What if" questions that are starting to plague my mind on the back burner for now.

It was as if God was speaking to me by making my mind shift to Dahlia. I couldn't put my finger on it, but something was wrong. So as I always do, I start to talk to God about her. "God, you have kept me and my sisters safe. I have yet to bury, bail, or sit with either of them at the hospital. And for that I'm so grateful. Thank you God. Dahlia is heavy on my mind and dear to my heart. If there is something I'm supposed to know to help her in any way, please tell me. I won't go on my own, I'll do exactly what you lead me to do. She's my sister, but she's your child. You know what's best for Dahlia. I trust you and your judgment."

I instantly felt peace. I knew God would take care of it. That is a feeling that I honestly can't describe. But I'm getting used to it. Salvation is so much more than what you can't do. For me it's the ability to relax and know that God will take care of it. As long as I put forth a valiant effort to make Him happy, He will take care of it all. To be able to truly relax is a luxury that most people never get to enjoy. "Thank You Jesus. Now back to the Adonis that you sent to the bar!" I laughed again. That man was mystic and beautiful. His skin was dark and smooth. He had the nerve to wear gray contacts. They were absolutely mesmerizing. He had a raised scar on his right bicep. I had to stop myself from running my fingertips over it. He had dreads that hit the middle of his back. They were jet black and freshly twisted. But the thing that set them off was the ends of his dreads were dyed gray to match his contacts. Simply perfect. He was dressed in a mint muscle shirt, dark wash denim jeans and mint, blue and white sneakers. Nothing fancy. But he caught my eye and my attention when he smiled. Touch Lord Touch!

"Okay God, what's going on with the dude? I mean he comes in and orders a drink, says a few pleasantries and then he drops that earth shattering phrase. On top of that, he smiles at me like he knew he rattled my cage. Then dude just walks off like it was nothing. Who does that?!" I suddenly got a cold chill. It hit me from the top to the bottom. Every time that happens I get nervous. I put both hands on the steering wheel and breathe slowly and deeply. I needed to brace myself for whatever comes next. And as if on cue, the phone rang. "Korede' speaking." I am sounding much more at ease and normal than I feel. "Korede'...your name is as beautiful as you are. Listen, I'm Nigel Hampton. You and I met last night at the club. Now please don't get upset about me having your number. It took quite a bit of sweet talking to get. But I was willing to do whatever I needed to. You and I need to talk, pretty lady." I suppressed a scream. "Can you hold on for just a moment?"

I didn't wait for an answer. I hit that button and the brakes at the same time. I pulled over to the shoulder and put the car in park. I screamed for a good 20 seconds. I had a thank you fit. I told God thank you for this man and whatever he needed to talk to me about. I think God was laughing at me. I would've been if I were Him. "Nigel, right? I'm sorry to put you on hold. You say we need to talk. How can I help you?" I hoped he couldn't hear me smiling.

"Korede' I'd like to take you out for dinner and discuss some private matters." His voice was flirty but serious.

"Well I just left town so can we reschedule for next week?" He paused. "Next week will be too late. What is out of town? An hour, maybe two?" What's the rush? I won't date anyone else, I swear. "An hour and a half due east." I heard him smile. It made my jaw crack as I opened my smile even wider. "I know that town. They have the best food at the Coop De Ville there. Can you meet me there tomorrow? Say noon?" No he didn't just say the same thing I was thinking when I got in the car. He gives me such good vibes. "Sure, I'll be there." I was going to ask why couldn't he just text it, but I wanted to see him. I love the way his lips move when he talks. "Alright Ms. Korede', I'll see you then." And he hung up the phone.

That was so weird, but so welcomed. I held the phone up to my chest and began to pray. "Father, if it be your will, let this man be the man for me in this season that I'm in. Allow him to build me up and not tear me down. Let him see the You in my character and not try to change who I am to fit his own agenda. God do your thing in me and him. I'll give you all the praise and glory. In Jesus' name...Amen." I immediately felt better. I was still excited, but it was calm. Like I was on a high. I laid the phone back in the console and continued my drive to Taco Bell. No need to eat 'Coop De Ville' two days straight.

Chapter

5

<u>Dahlia</u>

The drag of a black and mild is all I've been thinking about for the last 3 hours. It is soothing. Not only to my nerves but to my entire respiratory system. That first pull is a teaser. It allows your brain to get excited while it tempts your soul. The second inhale is the hook. If you can ever get to the second pull it'll have you smoking at least two a day. The third lung filling addictive burn is honestly when you stop feigning for a smoke. If you don't get to that third pull you'll be back at it in less than an hour feeling unfulfilled. "Paging D.D Emerley to the ER". Man...they know I'm trying to sneak in a smoke break! At least I got to the fifth inhale. I don't know why I'm upset, I love the hustle and bustle of the Emergency Room. I've had several offers to be in an office setting. I refused them all. That's just too slow for my personality. I like to be where the action is. Give me more than one thing to do. I begged God for this busy life.

As I headed back indoors, I got to thinking. Lately I just need a moment or two to myself but I never get it. I haven't been alone in a while. My thoughts are everywhere and they have been driving me crazy. I'm in love and never alone. So I don't know how I feel about it. "In Love" is a foreign concept that I honestly haven't gotten used to. I've been obligated, infatuated, obsessed, and even drove to the brink of insanity. But never in love. It's beautiful and scary. It's a contradiction of so many emotions. And the only people who understand are the people who have been in love but not any kind of love. The wrong kind of love. The one that makes your life a living hell. The kind that turns your insides out. The one that makes your whole world flip upside down. Love that's so good that it's addictive. But every addict will tell you that when the high is over, the pain and regret is unbearable. The thought pattern becomes shameful because you are only planning and thinking about the next adventure; which is high.

I was raised in church. I know what the bible says about my love. Honestly I don't care. I tried the bible's way on love and partners. It just didn't work for me. I will not live in misery all my life hoping that the great up yonder is so good that it makes up for all the suffering. When He moves in my direction in such a way that I give up my form of love, I will not fight him. Until then if not Traci, then there will be another young lady on my arm. I have made this seemingly good life for myself. I give God his due. I try to treat people right. Love my neighbor as myself. Give to those in need. Feed the hungry. Heal the broken and sick. I try to be a good person. I just love who I love. And it may not seem like it, but I love and respect God very much. I know His presence when I feel it. I haven't felt it in a while, a long while actually. I miss it.

My definition of romance is frowned upon, shunned, and unacceptable by most. You know you're letting someone down. But you know you're inspiring others as well to just love the way they love. The question is, is this inspiration worth its price? Being open and out has cost me so much. I lost family, friends, jobs, scholarships. Most of all, I lost my mother. She will not speak to me. She won't have anything to do with me. I see her from time to time in passing. I have to ask my brothers and some church members about her. The last time I saw my mom, she was unconscious. She was complaining of stomach pain. I was the only person on call that night. I'm a Surgical Care Nurse Practitioner with expertise in Emergency Medicine. So I'm the closest thing she had to true help. I performed an appendectomy on my own mama, who told me she hated that she didn't abort me. She said it would be better to have not had me at all than to have a bulldagger for a daughter.

After surgery all my brothers: David, Daylan, Dorian, and Damien were in the waiting room. Damien Marsalle, the baby, looked at me with tears in his eyes. He still stayed at home with mama at the time because it was the beginning of his junior year in high school. He's not allowed to talk to me or about me as long as he's in her house. He sneaks and calls me anyway. He lies to her and says he's going to the gym to play ball with the boys. He ends up on my doorstep for dinner. He stood up to hug me. He laid on my shoulder and wept. When he pulled himself together he asked, "Doll, is she dead?" He was so conflicted with emotions that they were just spilling over. "No bayboy. I did what had to be done. The surgery went perfectly. She will have a small scar on her belly. Aside from that, she'll be just fine. Make sure she goes to her family doc for all her follow up appointments. I've done all I can do. Y'all take good care of her. Tell her that a traveling physician performed her surgery when she asks."

When she woke up the next day, she asked my younger brother, Daylan Malik, what happened because she remembered nothing. He respected my wishes and told her that white lie. Unfortunately she pushed Damien over the edge in an argument three months later. He told her the whole truth as he packed his clothes to come move in with me. She told him she better never see him again. He told her it would be his pleasure. He said, "And when you finally die and God tells you that you're not welcomed in His kingdom, remember the children you refused to love and you'll know exactly why hell has a spot just for you. You're a piss poor excuse of a Christian and an even worse mother. When you see me in the streets, act like you don't know me. 'Cause that's exactly how I'mma act. Believe you me!"

All of my brothers are fine with me, with it. We eat together at one of our houses once a week. We keep in touch like family is supposed to. And because of that, they've lost their mother too. She won't deal with them either. They said "Don't worry about her. All she did was lie, mooch and complain. We're glad she's done with us. She wasn't a mama no way." But sometimes it still bothers me. If I wasn't the way I am would it make matters better? At least for them.

My mind is floating off into left field as it usually does while I'm listening to my patient's lung function as they breathe. The sound of someone breathing is so soothing to me. It reminds me of the scripture "Let everything that has breath praise ye the Lord." This 14 year old man has the flu, so he says. However the test came back negative. He does have a fever and he is definitely congested. "Okay. Your lungs are clear. The test is an ixnay on the flu."

In my game show announcer voice, "Tell him what he's won. You have the Crud! You're going home with your very own Z-Pak for infection, Ibuprofen for pain and fever, and Deconex for congestion prescriptions to be filled at your local pharmacy. Your cold and sinus medicine is accompanied by a school excuse as well as my advice to drink plenty of water. Please keep socks on your feet and have a hat on your head when you go out into the wind. The Crud is not contagious but I wouldn't recommend kissing your girlfriend or your grandma for at least the next week." He smiled, blushed, and giggled.

I handed the prescriptions to his father, who smiled and shook my hand with gratitude, and they left my consultation room. Children giggling at me makes me feel like I've done my job and done it well. I decided to become an ER Nurse Practitioner for the kids. I remember being in the hospital a lot when I was younger. They weren't good experiences. I got nasty looks and was treated roughly. I vowed to grow up and do it better than them. So, here I am at 32 fulfilling my promise to myself. And when I'm struggling to keep it together, God sends a kid in to make me remember why I do what I do.

"Black Brother, I love ya. And I will never try to hurt ya." My phone is telling me that one of my brothers is calling me now. That Angie Stone's got so much soul! She gave so much love through that song. "Hello?" "Yo Dolly, I'm at your crib. When are you coming home?" David Manuell Emerley, the oldest of the bunch. Responsible, single and one of my best friends. "Man, I don't get off work till the am. You gone have to watch the game and eat without me. And please don't tear my house up. Clean up after yourself. I'm not giving you talking room 'cause I can't talk. Gotta go homie. Peace" He was laughing the whole time I was talking. "Well Damn Doll. Bye then." I began to laugh after I hung up the phone.

He can be trusted to do any and everything for me, except clean up behind himself. But that's my brother though. All of them are that way except that last one. He suffers from OCD, thank God. One of them had to be. I mean I knew I couldn't be the only clean freak in the house of all those sport playing boys. I played too; basketball, point guard position. And I'll admit, playing against the boys made me into what I was. I mean hey, they didn't offer me three scholarships for nothing. I was a little above average on the court. I loved it. The trips, the girls, the noise talking. On those trips those girls became my family. We were and still are thick as thieves. We all ended up taking the same scholarships to the same junior college. Some were second string. All in all the old team dominated the court for the entire two years we were there. Now I'll admit all that noise talking got me into a few altercations outside of the gym. But it was worth every punch thrown and taken. Those were the good ol days. After that I got two scholarships to Mississippi University for Women. Between academic and athletic awards I was close to a free ride. I took it with a smile on my face and sadness in my heart. All my other teammates were accepted to University of Southern Miss or William Carey College in Hattiesburg and I was three hours away in Columbus. We met up one weekend a month and took a week vacation during the summer for years.

Now we just text each other when we have time and meet up one weekend out of the year. We've been at each other's graduations, weddings, baby showers, and divorce proceedings. It's amazing that I have three separate support systems; two that aren't even blood. I have God to thank for that. I lost my mother, but I gained so much more. She rejected a daughter. And because of that, she lost her sons. "D.D. Emerley to the O.R." I can't even fill out paperwork and think for a few moments. You know what? Lord thank you for the hustle and bustle of

an emergency room and the beautiful paycheck that goes along with it.

Chapter

6

<u>Liberty</u>

After spending the entire day in interviews, interrogations and photo shoots, officer good looking Calloway finally took me home. I will admit that I was so content just looking at him. One of the forms I was handed to fill out at the station had his full name on it. Adonis C Calloway Jr; his mother knew exactly what she was doing naming him that. I was very content watching him and allowing my thoughts, and imagination to run wild. But he wanted to talk. I'll keep up this pleasurable and polite façade. I'll talk. "So you from around here?" Small talk. Get to know you chit chat. Okay, I got you. "Yes, I was born and raised here in Columbia Mississippi. I graduated from Columbia High and went straight to the Army. What about you?" He smiled all smooth. "I'm not from around here. I was born in New Orleans, raised in Milwaukee, and graduated from junior college in Atlanta." My eyebrows went up.

I've been to all those places and some but only as an adult. He's spoken of his time before adulthood. "That's a lot of moving mister. Army brat?" He shook his head as he was driving, looking everywhere but me. "Pastor's kid. I was raised Methodist. They move their pastors around if so desired after only one year. I really don't think they consider the families of the preachers when these decisions are made. But it's just one of those things, you know?" I nodded my head.

Now I understood why I liked him. Aside from his body, I was attracted to his raising; his soul. He was brought up right. There is so much good in him. That makes no sense. I am not deserving of this kind of a man. I'm usually attracted to the wrong man. The one with the bad seed in his heart.

Obviously...God is telling me that it's time to change. It was then I began to feel self-conscious about the sinfulness and evil in my own heart. My mind immediately shifted to Dahlia. It occurred to me that it wasn't her lifestyle that prevented me from being happy for her. It was the selfishness settled in my own soul. I wasn't happy, so I refused to be happy for her.

She treated me a lot like God. No matter what I did or didn't do, she was right there to love me and make it better. Then my mind shifted back to God. Look how I've treated him while wearing his name. We don't talk like we used to. I haven't read my bible in a year. I go to church when I'm not too hung over from Saturday night living. I'm always begging for him to do something for me. "God if you get me out of this..." I'm infamous for that lie. I'm old enough to know better but too selfish to do it.

"Hey...why did you get quiet on me? You changed the whole mood in my car. What happened? What's on your mind?" Aw man... and he's perceptive! "Can I be honest with you?" He pulled in front of my house. Got out of the car. Came over to my side and opened the door like a gentleman. I got out and thought maybe he didn't want me to be honest. So I didn't say anything else and walked to my front porch with my key in my hand. I was going to turn around to holler back thanks for the ride home. When I turned around he was standing right behind me. I jumped. "Yes, you can be honest with me." I am usually very observant and alert.

Nothing gets past me. But because of my current thought pattern he caught me off guard. I was shocked that he was there. "Um..." I didn't want to be around anybody right now. I knew my eyes were full and I cry alone. But I couldn't stop them from spilling over. "Um..." My voice began to crack. The heat of emotion sat in my chest and burned. I just dropped my head. There was nothing that I could do to stop this train from speeding down the tracks. I took one deep breath and the floodgates opened.

In seconds I was wailing. Something inside me opened up and mourned. I tried to hide my face. However the regret, guilt, and hurt raged on and weakened me. He grabbed me before my legs gave way. He eased me down to the floor of the porch. He knelt in front of me. He held me. He prayed for me. I heard him; the words he was telling God on my behalf. Those words seemed to reach inside of my heart and offered explanations that I had no way of understanding. But they were so precise in meaning. I honestly felt as if my flesh was stripped away and this man could see my heart. I wasn't as uncomfortable as I wanted to be.

There are some things that only Dahlia knows; no one else. She is the only one who has been able to share in this grief, regret, and hell that has been my life. But here I am in the middle of a panic attack on my front porch wrapped in the arms of the pastor's son. My lifelong anxiety issues are making me forge a soul tie strong connection with a man I don't even know. I have no control over my body now. My breathing has become labored and I can't stop shaking. I'm having a hard time focusing. He simply helped me to my feet and took the keys from my hand. He had no issues holding me up with his right arm while he worked the door, key and lock with his left hand. I know he helped me in the house and led me to the bathroom. But it was as if I was watching from a distance. He put me in the tub, clothes on and all, and ran the shower.

The coldness of that water shocked me into a better breathing pattern. It calmed me down enough to come back into my own consciousness and take some semblance of control. He was caring and careful. His touch was strong and soothing. He grabbed a towel out of the cabinet and wrapped it around me. He was humming. It was a song that I had never had the privilege of hearing. But it took pleasure in soothing my soul and taming this beast of emotion roaring in my chest. His voice was anointed. He was anointed. So much so that I became afraid. My selfishness and need for attention had pushed me to think of this man in gutter ways. God! How far off the path am I? If I allow this thought pattern to continue I would end up back in the tub with cold water beating down on me.

"What's the name of the song you're humming?" He looked into my eyes for the first time since I got out of his car. "In The Garden." His words were simple but so full of love and care. I just nodded. Not sure of what to say next. He sat on the floor in the hall and beckoned for me to sit with him. I sat in between his legs. He wrapped a new towel around me and held me from behind. He gently rocked me from side to side. He began to sing the words to the song. I can't explain it. The tears came in a steady flow. But it wasn't the same as before. Before I was a bad girl who was getting punished.

Now, I'm a woman who has to make the decisions to change. But it has to be done now. I feel if I wait for tomorrow, it'll be too late. The mistakes I've made in my life are mine to answer for. And they were demanding their answer now. The truth of my existence had been avoided like the plague. Truth is I was created for God and his use. I haven't been acting like it. As a matter of fact I've been living as though His rules didn't apply to me. I now have to come and reason with myself and my actions, my thinking, my heart. I have always known deep in my heart that I was going to get a good whipping.

I have been so angry with God. Why would such a loving God allow such harsh damage to be done to me? What did I do for him to hate me so? Why did I need to be punished for being born to the wrong people? He hasn't really given me an explanation. He's God. He doesn't really owe me one. When I go to the end of my wits, He sends someone along to calm the storm. Usually that person is Dahlia. She sits me down and fixes it enough for me to carry on. Today it's good looking Calloway in the hot seat.

Okay God, I'm tired of this cycle. Before I knew it and without my consent my head was in the crook of his neck. And after a long and intense battle I surrendered to a God who I knew was giving me my last chance. All my fears and stubbornness were laid on the altar of my heart. I relinquished control of my life, my heart, and even my emotions. I stopped harboring hatred for my mother and my father. I stopped judging other people's mistakes for the purpose of making me look better. I handed over my selfishness and self-righteousness. I allowed God to tear down the wall I built between us. I didn't want to be strong willed and hard headed anymore.

Lord Adonis...I think he knew what was going on inside of me. While the war was raging inside of my heart and mind, he never stopped singing; never stopped rocking. He was steady, stable, and reliable in this come to Jesus meeting. I guess that's all I needed for him to be. But I'll admit this isn't my idea of the perfect way to meet. After a while the tears stopped. My breathing came easy and no longer labored. The heart's beat returned to a normal rhythm. For the first time in 15 years, I felt normal without medication.

I leaned up on my own and turned to face him. "Adonis, I'm sorry I 'lost it' on you. I do want to thank you for being here through it all. You don't know how much peace your singing brought me. And please, don't think I'm completely crazy." He took my face in his hands and wiped away the stray tears with the pads of his thumbs. "Liberty, I don't know you enough yet to call you crazy." Without a filter, as usual, my mouth spoke before my brain could process the thought completely. I raised my right eyebrow and tilted my face down towards his, "Yet?" A sneaky grin snuck across his face. "Yes ma'am Ms. Liberty. Yet. Believe me when I tell you, I will get to know you." Mmm! Okay God, work it for my good then. Just as I was about to get off the floor he pulled me to him. "You will be alright. I will make sure of it." He kissed me on the cheek.

I think God is testing me. Will I renege on my surrender? Or will I keep true to my word? Let me prove it to myself. I looked him in his eyes, "I'll hold you to it, handsome. But for now, I need to shower and get warm before I catch a cold." I got off the floor and held out my hand to help him up. He took it with a smile on his face. I pulled him up. "Liberty Talbert, I'll leave my card on your table. Please text me before you go to sleep." I grabbed my robe and walked him to the door. "I will Adonis. And thank you for everything, really." He turned and looked at me before he walked out my door.

"You're very welcome. Call me Junior. That's what everybody who knows me calls me. So you should too." He walked off my porch and got in his car while I stood at my door grinning like a nut. I pulled the robe around me tight like an old woman. Once I was back inside, I laughed to myself. It's just like God to break me down and point me towards the light at the end of the tunnel on the same day. I need to talk to somebody. But not just anybody, somebody who will understand. Dahlia is at the hospital, but that's the main person I need to call. I have some apologizing to do. I haven't been much of a friend to her in about 6 months or so. Plus she will totally understand.

Chapter

7

<u>Chevy</u>

Now it's only been a few days since I've had that pep talk with myself on the dance floor. Leave the liquor and live the life you really want. Now I'm sitting in the middle of a whole lot of paperwork wishing I had a bottle of anything other than water. I'm cleaning my house; ridding myself of my dead husband and the mess he left behind. There are so many things I didn't know about that decided to come to light once he ascended into the darkness. I know what you're thinking. I have no right to judge anyone.

But what I did know about the bastard was that he had no regard for God or living right. And judging by this paperwork of insurance policies and deeds to houses I don't know anything about he didn't have much regard for his wife either. I have found six different insurance policies that do not list my name as the beneficiary, but different women in different states. I was wondering who certain people at the funeral and wake were. No wonder why they were crying harder than me. They lost their meal ticket.

I'm not able to have children. So I figured he'd go and make a baby with some fertile Myrtle; someone to carry on his name and features. But I didn't know the man went and made four babies. Such short and handsome sons too. I met all of them right before the funeral. You couldn't hide it because they looked like he spit each one of them out himself. I hugged every last one of them. Told them if they wanted to know more about their dad to call me. They mamas didn't like that.

I told them they might as well get over it. Ain't no use in fighting over a dead man. You knew he was married before you laid up with him. If he'd cheat on his wife, what about his mistress? I got some sense. I knew he was stepping out. I stopped sleeping in the same room with him. We were still cool and all; great roommates even. But he wasn't touching this pot because I knew "Winnie the Pooh" was stirring up in some other woman's honey.

I've been sober these last three days. I decided to stay sober by keeping busy. I started making gift boxes for his four sons. They all play basketball, baseball, and are smart as a whip just like their pops. So I thought they'd like having some of his old stuff; yearbooks, letterman's jackets, old jerseys, baseball gloves, hats, knives and pictures. God knows I don't want it. I was there. Memories are good enough for me. I wanted the guns and the money. That's it. I loved him, just not as a wife would love a husband.

It was the way he died that rocked me. They didn't just kill him. He was tortured; the officers said for days. They left his burned, cut, shot up body on the back porch. I found him. That's the reason I drank so heavily. I wanted to forget what I've seen. But I can't let him control me in his dying if I wouldn't allow him to rule me in his living. I've always been independent. I've always had my own back. He tried it. He would keep tabs on me. Tell me what he thought I should do. Where I should go. He didn't trust certain people I hung with. He hated my crew.

He said that I gave them more attention than I gave him. I told him that he was grown and so was I. If he wants to lead, do it by example. Don't tell me that he didn't like my girls when he won't let me meet his. He said my mouth was going to get me in trouble. I said that my hands could get me out of any trouble my mouth got me into. I'd give him a dangerous smile and go into another room. When he was high he'd follow me and get rough with me. But he knew that I'd fight him and pull out this gat. He'd back up every time.

The doorbell rang and pulled me out of my memory. I asked Michelle to come and pick up a box for her son, Sir Adrian McComb-Davidson. At 14, he's the oldest of all the boys and she's the calmest of all the mamas. "Hi, Shevelle. How are you holding up?" Why does that question piss me off so? I've got to work on that. She was just asking a question that honestly makes perfect sense. I just lost my husband to a gruesome crime.

"Hey Michelle. I'm alright. How are you?" She looks down at the ground and twists her foot like she's a little girl that doesn't want to tell the truth. "I'm pretty good." "Come on in. I've got bottled water." She comes through the door smelling sweet. She's a very pretty girl. She's about 5'6, the color of a caramel cake with brown freckles over her smooth skin. She had to have been about 140, maybe 145 pounds on a pms day. She works out. Her arms are toned. Straight pearly white teeth. But there's a shyness to her that makes you think she's younger than what she is. She has microbraids. I haven't seen them in years. But she wears them well.

As she walked to the kitchen, it dawned on me, that's all she was when she had Adrian; a girl. She couldn't have been no more than 15 when she had him. That bastard! How could he mess with a child! That's all she was! I have no filter regardless of whether I'm drinking or not. "Michelle, talk to me about something." She looked at me with big pretty brown eyes, "Yes ma'am?" "How old were you when you had Adrian?" She averted her eyes to the cabinets behind me. I knew the answer to my question right then. She whispered in shame, "14". I got so mad I started to cry right there in front of her. She didn't know what to do. She wanted to hug me, but she was scared to move. I had to compose myself. "Michelle?" I was still shaking in the voice. It's not that people don't get pregnant and have babies at 14. But it was my "husband" who did this to an impressionable young girl.

She started to spill the tea. "Shevelle, I was young and fast. I was trying to be grown and be something I wasn't. Truth is, it's' just as much my fault as it is his. Don't be angry Shevelle. The past can't be fixed. That's what I tell Adrian. It's the future that you can mold. I know this isn't the most glamorous story. But it is what it is. I hated him and me for what had taken place. But I wouldn't trade the world for Adrian." I just sat down on the floor in my kitchen. I was so stunned. If he was alive, he wouldn't be for much longer. I'd kill him myself.

Once I found my voice, I had so much to say. "First off, call me Chevy. Only the receptionist at the doctor's office calls me Shevelle. Secondly, I want to apologize for the behavior of my husband. I partly feel like it's my fault. Michelle, I'm barren. If I do my math correctly, that's around the time we found out that I won't be a biological mother to anyone. But he didn't have to do that to you. I'm sure you didn't give it up on the first day you met him. So his sick ass courted you and pursued after you. He hunted you. He knew how old you were. He might not have known the exact age. But he could tell by your voice and your eyes that you weren't over 18. He preyed on you. You didn't deserve that. UGHHHHHAAAHHHH!"

I was so enraged I couldn't control the scream that escaped from my soul or the beating of a war drum that happened to be my fist on the floor. She just nodded through her tears. It was at that moment that I began to feel hatred towards my husband. I began to understand why he died the way he did. He was, for lack of better words, a sick son of a bitch. I'm starting to wish I was the one the police were looking for. I'm also starting to wonder what else I was going to find out about the man I promised before witnesses to love, cherish and obey.

"Thank you Shevelle. I mean Chevy. No one has ever said that to me. My parents told me how much of a slut I was. My pastor told me that I was a disappointment. My sister told me that she was proud of me last year when she came home for the first time since Adrian was 4. She said he turned out alright as though she felt I'd fail at loving and raising my own son. Everyone has doubted me. Called me names behind my back and to my face. I started in the projects; just me and my son. We now live in a four bedroom house in a gated community. I went from being a single mom in high school to the owner and boss lady of my own hospice service.

The man who said he loved me and made a baby with me wouldn't even come to see me. He just dropped off money once a month. He made sure I had a cell phone. He said that when he called I'd better answer. Once when Adrian was three, Dade paid me an unexpected visit. He came through the door and demanded I give him some. I told him no. I was done with him and his games. The money he was giving me was for our son. I wasn't using it for any other purpose. He threw me up against the wall. My first cousin was in my room trying to fix my air conditioner. He came down the hall with his gun. My cousin is Cajun and he made Dade back up and go out the door, but not before he gave him a slap across the face with his rings on. That is where the scar under his left eye came from." I gasped. "He told me that he was in a car accident. He said that the cab he took when he was in New Orleans wrecked. And my dumb ass believed him."

She smiled through her tears. "I'm glad I wasn't the only one who believed his lies. I'm sorry for you too, Chevy. You didn't sign up for this life. He had his way with all of us. He was evil. He had a way about himself that pulled you in despite the little voice inside telling you to run the other way. At least you had some fight in you. I heard how you stood up to him. I heard how you'd fight him back. I started taking self-defense courses when I heard that." I looked at her with so many questions.

"Don't be angry, I used to work at the same hospital as your friend. D.D Emerley is one of the best nurse pracs I know. She's the coolest person I've ever worked under. You know she still refers patients to my office for services? It's because of her that my business is booming as well as it is. But she'd tell us how proud she was of you and a few other women. How you'd do whatever needs to be done to take care of each other and yourselves. She told us how Dade had to come to the hospital to be treated for the ribs you broke. I was so glad I didn't work that night!" She was talking to me, but she had looked off at my cabinets again. She really was a sweetheart. She was a little girl my husband forced into womanhood. I wonder if her father, brother, best friend, or first cousin killed him. If so, I'd love to hug them and say "good job".

"Dee has always been there for me. I would've loved to have met you and Adrian earlier than I did. I wish she would've told me about you and him." She took her eyes off the counters and cabinets behind me and looked me dead in the eyes. "She had no idea that I had a son until his father's funeral. I kept him a secret from as many people as I could. People tend to think that you're irresponsible or incapable of making good decisions when they see you have a son half your age. I needed that job to provide for Adrian. I started throwing money back in Dade's face. I told him that was enough. I didn't want him to think that he was paying a high priced hooker for sex with his yellow envelopes. I also told him to stay away from me and my son. That's when I noticed him showing up at games and school programs. It's like when I finally started to want him dead, he started paying attention to the fact that he had a son."

I was glad to know she had a backbone. I feel like she could be my little sister of sorts. I could take her and be a part of her support system. I'm not sure how I feel about seeing Adrian yet. He looks so much like his father it's uncanny. I'm not committing to anything. But I'd rather deal with her than the other wide hipped heifers with attitudes he picked to procreate with. "Okay. Well you've knocked the wind out of me. Michelle, I'm sorry Dade picked you. But I'm glad that I get to know you. If there's something you need, or something Adrian needs let me know." She looked off while I talked. But as soon as I took a breath, she said.

"There's one thing. If, and it's a big if, Dade left any money for Adrian can you put it in a college fund for him. I've been so busy trying to survive that I didn't realize that college is right around the corner. I really don't want to take out a loan for him to go to the University of Southern Miss. He's got his heart set on it. That's where his 'Daddy' graduated. That's all he's been talking about since the funeral. That obituary is the most he's ever known about him."

"If there's anything he wants to know about him, I'll tell him. And I won't talk bad about him to Adrian. But I will tell the truth. I am still going through all the paperwork and insurance policies. I'm not sure who half of these people are. A good friend of mine is coming home. She's a paralegal and she'll help me sort through a lot of it. She looked down at me and smiled.

"Thank you Chevy. I better be going. I've got to go pick up Adrian from ball practice." I got up from the kitchen floor. "Let me get you Adrian's package. I'm trying to get rid of some, okay all of Dade's things. I figured his boys would like some of his stuff." I handed her a heavy box full of memories that I can't wait to forget. She said her thank yous and she left. I was left there to consider burning down the house and every memory and bad deed in it.

Damn it! I need a bottle!

Chapter

8

<u>Byrd</u>

Coop De Ville sees me every other weekend. But this time it will see me with a good looking man. A great looking man. Ooh I'm so excited I don't know what to do! I did everything I could to look like a lady. But I didn't want to seem desperate. I dressed in peep toe heels, blue jeans, halter blouse, and a blazer. I thought it showed enough interest but not too much skin. Liberty said not to overdo it. Make it simple. But as simple as I made it, I'd still attract attention. No one ever sees me around with a guy, unless it's one of Dahlia's brothers. I want to make sure he and I sit in the back booth where no one nosey can keep interrupting our conversation. Something deep inside is nervous about the awaiting topic. It may be because I don't know what it is.

When I walked in the door, 10 minutes early, I looked around for the seat I wanted. And there he sat. Looking like heaven wrapped in flesh. My heart skipped a beat and my lungs refused to take in air. Kamdyn Korede Byrd...you better get it together. Or this beautiful man will be picking you up off the floor and rushing you to the ER. I spoke a silent prayer begging God to let me not seem desperate. I hate to be looked at like a little girl. So I try so hard not to act like one.

"You are unspeakably beautiful Ms. Korede." He said as he rose from his seat to greet me. He had on a nice gray button down with dark wash jeans with the faded thigh and gray Nikes. Lord please don't let me be grinning like a fat kid at a bakery, please? "Looking like a million dollars yourself Mr. Nigel. How are you feeling?" I said as I extended my hand. He took my hand and shook it while his eyes never left mine. God, you have taken over my mind and mouth.

Cause I thought I lost all sense of vocabulary. "I'm well. Okay, I'm nervous as hell." He smiled a smile; a cat ate the canary smile. It was cute. But nothing he could do would be ugly.

"Don't be nervous. Let's just talk." I wouldn't let him know I could've peed all over myself cause I was so nervous. He gestured that I have a seat. I did. He said, "Before we talk, I just want to say that this is not my usual behavior. I have to speak some business with you, but I want to appeal to your softer side as well. I find you appealing. Not only your looks, which took my breath away. But you have good sense and sensibility. So I have a double reason for meeting you here today. Don't allow one to affect the other, okay?" All of a sudden I felt the chills...the chills that warn me that I need to pay full attention to what's in front of me. "Okay. I'm all ears. Shoot."

"I'm originally from Louisiana. I know things. I've done things that I shouldn't have. I ended up being in other people's business in ways I wished I wasn't. I've left wrong alone. I have come to Jesus. I've changed my ways. I begged God to give me the chance to right my wrongs. If not all of them, at least one. This is my chance, you understand?" I just nodded my head and motioned with my hands so that he would continue.

"My half-brother has a wife, we call her Tracie. She came to me with an issue. She wanted to get something and she paid me, well, to help her obtain it. I told her what supplies I needed to help her. She got them. So I did what I was paid to do." I held up my hand for him to stop. "What did you need to get the job done?" He looked down at his hands for a moment. "A lock of their hair, something with the person's name on it that they've touched, and three red roses from that person's home town." I held up my hand again.

I wanted to get up and run. This man did magic. I don't do people who do voodoo. At that moment my body filled with cement. For the life of me I couldn't get up. I wanted to run screaming and hollering from that booth. What was I thinking?! This couldn't have been God. I need to get the hell out of here. "See I..." I held up my hand again. I needed to process everything, including why I couldn't move. And why he's telling me. Lord...I'll kill him I swear I will. I go nowhere without this gun within reach. But I keep feeling these chills like I need to pay attention.

Not trusting my mouth, I motion for him to continue his story with my hands. "I did magic, mostly dark magic. I don't do it anymore. But there was something different about Tracie's situation. I made it a habit of writing down all my 'sessions' with all my clients so I would have proof if anything went sideways. I went back and read this particular entry a few months ago. I prayed and begged God to let me fix this one. Some things that were said and done were harmful intentions toward a young lady. I went to social media and found her pages. She's beautiful, smart. I didn't want any harm to come to her. So I stalked her pages and memorized everybody's faces I could. You popped up on her page. So when I saw you at the bar not far from where my nephew goes to school I felt it was my answered prayer. Now don't get me wrong, I came three times before I got the courage to come and say anything to you. And I had to ask God to guide my words. I had no idea what to say."

He stopped and took a sip of sprite. He must have known I needed a minute to soak it all in. He opened his mouth to speak again. I stopped him. "I need some food. I'm not running away, yet. But If I'm going to hear you out, I need food and drink and quite possibly some liquor. I'm taken by surprise...and that's putting it mildly. So hold that thought, and let me get some of this smoked brisket and some potato salad. Okay?" He just nodded and stood up as I scooted out of the booth. While I stood in line to get my plate, I noticed that my pastor's daughter was in front of me. She's much older than me. She's a dynamic preacher. She's also a prophet. I started to wonder what's the difference between what she does and what Nigel does? He used his for evil. She uses hers for good. If he's right now, what's the difference between them? Who's to say that she didn't start out like him? And what if he turns out like her?

"Byrd! You couldn't stay away from my cooking could ja gal?" Old Mrs. Juanita Winston greeted me as she fixed my plate. That's the thing about being in familiar territory. I didn't have to tell her what I wanted. She just knew. "No ma'am Mrs. Winston. You know I couldn't. You've been doing alright?" She smiled at me. It was a knowing smile. Something about it made me feel like I was at home. I don't get that often. "I do's alright baby. You keep on keepin' on at that schoolhouse, hear?" When she said hear, she said it with such force that it made her round belly jump. I tilted my head down a bit to remind me of my manners. I smiled at her and said, "Imma make you proud Mrs. Winston. I promise."

She nodded her head towards me and said, "That's what I'm talkin' bout. I hear ya Byrd!" She put the biggest smile on my face. I went to pay for my food at the cash register. I was once again behind the pastor's daughter. She turned to me and said "I heard you were in college...studying law, right?" I was shocked she even knew who I was. I just nodded. "Good for you. Good luck. And just know when times get tough and you want to run, God knows exactly what He's doing." She winked at me and walked off. I had to stop myself from flopping my mouth open. I needed that in the worst way and it had nothing to do with school. I slid my plate up to the cash register. I usually small talk with the cashier. He's Mrs. Winston's grandson. He's sweet and shy. But with all the information given to me today, all I could do was tell Jasper hello. "Byrd, the man you been talking to already paid for your lunch. You can gone and eat." I told him thank you and headed back to the table. The feeling of fight or flight was beginning to leave. A peace that made no sense fell over me. "Okay God. Okay", I whispered before I got within earshot of Nigel.

I shook my head at him when he tried to stand up before I sat down. I got it, he's a gentleman. He doesn't have to prove it by tipping his hat at every woman he sees. He's a diamond. Seems to be inside and out. I took a sip of the too sweet tea and prayed for my kidneys. "Okay Nigel. Let's say I understand. I believe you. What is it exactly do you expect me to do to help you right a wrong?" Cause honestly, I take pictures with a lot of people. It could be a person I only met once on a Friday night at work. That person might not remember me.

"Korede', this client was intent on killing this young lady. I just want you to help me figure out how to make sure this lady is safe." "Okay. I'll try." "I'm sure you will. Once you find out who the young lady is you'll probably go above and beyond." I hate when people who just met me feel like they know me. "Really...who is it and let's see if I even remember them. Cause you've got to understand, I see a lot..." "Korede', it's Dahlia Emerley."

My world broke. I don't mean it stopped. I mean it broke. I couldn't hear. My sight was fuzzy. I felt like there was a fan blowing gusts of wind in my face. I couldn't breathe. I started to sweat. My heartbeat was out of control. He did say the name Tracie at the beginning of the conversation. The woman that D said she was going to bring to church Sunday is Tracie. Now I'm beginning to get dizzy. Next thing I know, Nigel has something cold pressed against my neck. I can feel the warmth of his hand in mine. He whispered my name in my ear. It sounded foreign coming from his mouth. I could hear his accent. He said it louder. "Hmm." That's as good as it was gonna get for a while. I couldn't get my bearings. "Beautiful, breathe in through your nose slowly and out through your mouth. Be easy with it. Let's get you to feeling like yourself again, okay?" I nodded. Nothing I was doing was working. So I might as well obey his instructions. I closed my blinded eyes and did just what he said. About a minute later I felt so much better.

I opened my eyes and tears fell without my consent. I opened my mouth to speak but I could feel the rush of emotion about to make me have an ugly cry. So I just shut it. "You just concentrate on your breathing, Beautiful. Everything else will calm right down. I promise you." I closed my eyes again to do just what he said. And true to his words, I was getting closer to normal. I opened my eyes to look at him. He was scooting to get out of the booth with me so he could sit back on his side. "Don't go. You can stay." He looked at me with a smile on his face. He looked relieved. "I'm glad you're okay." "I'd love to know what just happened." "You had a panic attack. Judging by your reaction, that's your first one. I hope it's your last." "Hmm...you're not the only one." He touched my hair. Now usually, that's a no no. Okay that's an "Aw Hell Naw" moment. But I wanted to be in this man's arms with the way that I was feeling. I felt like I had been running in a bad dream.

But there was someone out there who wanted my best friend, my sister hurt. She had gotten very far. Too far. As far as I'm concerned, this is a bad dream. She had to be stopped. "Nigel what do we do? And please don't tell me you need a frog's leg, a drop of blood and one of D's fingernail clippings to stop this." He laughed. "I'm out of that game Korede'. I promise. It will take some talking, some proof, and some love to stop what Na'Treiel is up to.

Chapter

9

<u>Dahlia</u>

"What's happening baby?" Ugh...I hate it when men catcall. I'm feminine. I'm the epitome of a girl. Dolled up, heels, nails done, hair done, smell good; girly. I can just run a ball and fight. It's not that I don't like men. I do. Very much so. I just haven't found one worth liking in a while. I used to be the one night stand type. But I think there comes a time when you outgrow that phase. Now I believe everyone should have that phase of life. Be careful and have fun. Tonight, I'm not in the mood for fun. I just want my food and a very hot shower. As soon as I walk in the restaurant, in scrubs no less, I catch the eye of someone that I wish was blind. Lesson to all men, have some class when you approach a woman; PLEASE! Catcalling is just as bad as or worse than being called out of our name.

"Say ma...let me play doctor wi'chew duhnight." I acted like I didn't hear a word. That is the lamest line I've heard in years. I wanted to laugh but that might encourage him to keep on talking. The cashier was snickering at him. I handed the young lady a twenty and told her to keep the change. I wanted to get out of there as fast as possible. I managed to get to the door before he started again. "C'mon ma!? I got whatcha need ri'chea. Don't lee me lonely ni." That Mississippi slang was thick on that drunk tongue. I looked at him as hard as I could and rolled my eyes. He finally got the point and let it go. That's the third time I've been hit on this week. Most men I get attention from are either under the age of 10 or over the age of 60. There is usually no in between. Lately the 20-40 year olds have been putting in their bid. That so and so in the restaurant had to have been in his early 40's. I wonder why the tables are turning all of a sudden. It must be because I'm happy. I'm not looking for love. Love has finally found me. I am happy with Tracie.

Although I will admit that I'm becoming someone I don't like when I'm with her. I'm whiny and needy. That's not me. I'm also worried about what she'll think if I do this or say that. That's not me either. It's as if I like her so much I don't want to offend her in any way. But people are people. Offenses will happen with or without our knowledge or consent. Now the oddity comes into play when I realize that I'm in love with what I'm presented with. Not what actually is. The interactions between us are amazing. But the unknown is troubling. There is no doubt that there is a whole lot of love between us. Blind Bartimaeus could've seen that. It just something is off and I need to figure out what it is. But honestly, I don't want to figure it out. Especially if it means finding out the worst about someone I feel like I can't live without. It is something Liberty is just going to have to get used to. I love Lib. She's my best friend; my sister. I love her so much and it kills me that she put me in this position. I know it's gonna come down to me choosing between the two greatest women in my life. And I don't want to make any decisions like that.

My thoughts have consumed me so much that I drove right past my place and right into Liberty's driveway. I saw the sheriff's car in her yard and I got very nervous. I completely forgot about the food in the car and the fact that I'm truly exhausted from a 12 hour shift. I left the car on, opened the car door and ran with all I had left to her front door. I'm banging on the door like I just know she's dead. Marsha Ambrosius' song "Far Away" started to play all loud inside my head. "So sad to see you go so soon. I know that you ain't coming back." I started to cry despite myself. "Lib! Liberty! OPEN THIS DOOR!" And the door opened. A familiar face appeared in the doorway. The officer was standing there smelling like coffee. He had a concerned look on his face. I was wondering if he was thinking how hard it was going to be to tell me that my ace was dead.

"Ma'am...come on in. Liberty is in her room getting dressed. She's fine, I promise. I just stopped by before my shift started to see how she was doing. Don't just stand out there, come on in." He was well trained. He did his best to calm me down. But I'm still wondering how he, a cop, knew her. I stepped into the living room with my sights set on her bedroom. I bust right through the closed door. When I saw her pinning up her hair, I rushed over to her and hugged her so tight. The tears fell down like a pouring rain. I had one of those sobbing, heaving and hoeing cries. She just held on to me and allowed me to cry. About three minutes later she held me back at arm's length. "Dahlia Dacieon Emerley, what has gotten into you?" She was just a wiping my face like she was my mother. "Are you alright?" That's all I managed to get out. She smiled at me in a motherly tone of voice. "I'm just fine. If anything were to happen to me you know you'd be the first to know. I'm alright Dahlia." I was able to slow the sobs. But the tears kept falling. I couldn't manage another word. I didn't trust myself to say anything. At that moment I understood which girl I'd choose if it came down to a choice that had to be made. Family is everything.

"Now what made you think I wasn't alright?" For some reason the professional in me took over. I saw the signs of abuse all over her. "It might be the officer in your living room or the bruises on your face and arms." She looked at me dead in my face with strength and peace that I've never seen in her possession. "I had a fight with the married boyfriend. I scared him to death with the gun and broke up with him. I'm just fine D. I was going to tell you everything you needed to know after you woke up from your nap this evening. Now, you need some rest. I suggest you go grab that guest room and get you some. I was led just like a puppy. That's something else I'm not happy about. Before meeting Tracie, I was the leader. I did what I wanted to do. People followed me. Now, I'm doing as I'm told. I thought it was me submitting to love, but now I'm not so sure.

I walked out of Lib's room and was going to cut off my car. "Oh, I put your keys and your food on the kitchen counter. It smells so good. You got one clean car Ms. Emerley. You make me wanna go car shopping. Now, I hope you have a great morning. Liberty, can I talk to you for a minute on the porch?" The officer spoke in a caring and smooth manner. I know him from work; bringing people in and taking statements and such. But there weren't many interactions between the two of us.

"D, go shower. You look a mess and I don't want that infection you treated in my sheets." Liberty smiled at me. I knew she was serious though. She is borderline OCD too. Again, I just did as I was told. As I went to bathe, I saw Mr. Officer hug Lib in a protective way that warmed my heart. I was happy for her. He was displaying all the right qualities. I'll still watch him though. I know it wasn't him that hit her. When Lib's pulls out that gun, she's done. My phone goes off and reminds me that I'm in my thoughts staring in the mirror. I'm so out of it, I forgot to get in the tub. "Sup?" "Baby, where are you?" Did I forget dinner with Tracie or something? "I'm at Liberty's. Why? What's up?" I sensed some agitation in her voice. "You were supposed to come home after work. You didn't tell me you weren't coming home." And for the first time ever in our relationship, the realness of Daecion came forth. "And...what bill of mine do you pay to have such authority in my life sugar?"

She was taken back but didn't back down. "You didn't tell me of any plans that you have today. Including your brother being in the kitchen cooking and staying for the game. You could have told me Dahlia. You're usually much more responsible than this." She was slick snapping on me for the goings on in MY house. "Yeah, you need a minute." I hung the phone up in her face.

I immediately called David's cell. "Doll, you coming home?" I'm trying to calm my emotions. "Bruh, are you the only one in my house?" He started turning off the eyes on the stove. You can hear the knobs clicking. If I know him, he cooked a breakfast fit for a royal family. "Yeah. Why you ask?" My face frowned as I stepped in the tub. "Tracie just called upset that I didn't tell her I wasn't coming home and that you were there. But if she's not there, how did she know you were in the kitchen cooking?" If I know my brother, he got that glock in the back of his pants. Military trained him well. "I'll make sure everything is secure and call you back 'cause you and I gotta talk. Holla."

After I hung up the phone, heaviness fell on me so hard that my legs gave way in the tub. Try as I might, getting up alone wasn't going to happen. There was a darkness pulling at me. The quiet and comfort. The emotional toil I usually feel is gone. The whispers and sneers of others faded away. Opinions of the insignificant were replaced with pure nothingness. No matter what I did or thought about, I wasn't strong enough to fight it off. I closed my eyes against my will. It felt so good. I will never be able to describe how good it felt to not fight it. I can hear Liberty just waltzing into the bathroom and yapping like everything is fine. When she didn't hear me fussing at her to let me bathe in peace, she immediately snatched the shower curtain open.

"Oh no ma'am Whitney Houston. Not in my house." Leave it to Liberty. The things that come out of her mouth at the oddest times. She turned off the water and dried me off. All I could do was grunt. I didn't have it in me to move or form real words. "Dahlia, I'm going to get you out of this tub and into the bed. I'm sure I can pick you up. You've lost quite a few pounds. We gotta talk when you can actually respond." What is it about everybody gotta talk all of a sudden? What is it that everybody thinks they see that needs their attention?

Chapter

10

<u>Liberty</u>

God is really working in my life, and rather quickly might I add. There is a peace in my heart that has never been. I am far from having it together, but I feel better about life. I was thinking how long will it last? "Do right" has always been easy speaking and hard doing. I have been doing a lot of talking to God and a lot of cleaning. I cleaned out my closets, bathroom cabinets, phone contacts and messages. I cleaned out my soul. I want better. I want true and permanent change.

Dahlia showed up on my front porch at the same time Adonis stopped by to make sure I knew his intentions made me see God was putting the right people in my life to support me in doing life right for once. I will admit D's emotional state pulled out some type of maternal instinct. And I know I'm nobody's mama. I'll fight for a kid, but I am clueless on how to raise one. But I just needed to make sure she was alright. Usually the roles are reversed. I'm the one with the dripping face and the unruly emotions. I'm just glad I can be there for her once. But there is something really going wrong with D. The fear in her eyes when she burst through the door was alarming. D is the most fearless person I've ever known. She is the one who assures everyone that everything will be okay. She's a real life Olivia Pope. Something has her shook and I will find out what it is and fix it for her.

Adonis is becoming my backbone. We've known each other less than 48 hours and I've come to rely on his quiet strength. He's so wise and loving. He's so understanding and patient. I'm sure that this is God's doing, and as the scripture says, it is marvelous in my eyes; literally. As I walked in from the meeting on the porch. The words that Adonis said kept playing in my head; "You have everything you need to be the person you want to be. So the question is, who do you want to be?"

I heard the thud in my bathroom. I knew something was wrong. But I wanted to be the fixer, not the one to panic. When I walked into that bathroom, I smelled sulfur. That's an odd smell. That's not a normal occurrence in my house or Dahlia's. Lord...what is going on?! "Uh, is that some new drug on the market or something? I'm used to weed, but I don't know what this is." That's when I saw her hand hanging out the tub like she was taking a bath. But the shower water was running. I snatched that curtain because I was upset. I felt like there was a threat in my house. Madea said there's only two places a person can have peace; your house and the grave. I felt like something was threatening the peace in my house. Just as I was getting my life together, she was allowing hers to fall apart. Not on my watch. "No ma'am Whitney Houston! Not in my house!"

I dried her off and noticed how small she'd gotten. D has never been thick, but she ain't never been boney either. I have never seen her this small. The only time this girl lost weight was when she was stressed out from studying for her exam for national certification and working as a respiratory therapist full time. Other than that, ol girl can put away some food. She eats like there's no tomorrow. For her to be this small means there are some serious underlying issues going on with my good friend that she ain't telling nobody. I'm going to fix that when she's in condition to talk. Right now the only thing she's doing is grunting and frowning. I picked her up and carried her to the bed. But that smell of sulfur was getting louder. Now when I was a little girl, the pastor said if you smell sulfur there is a demon at work close by. My sister is in deep. I just don't know what she's in! Here I am racking my brain. I'm coming up with nothing because I haven't been too involved in her life lately. The last six months or so, I've been to myself. Selfishly, I've been into me and only me. We've spoken when need be or to keep up appearances for the whole of the group. But I've put everybody who would hold me accountable out of my business. Just as I put D under the covers in the guest bedroom, her phone rings. The Caller ID indicates it's the oldest of her brothers.

"David, it's Liberty. Dahlia isn't feeling well right now. You want me to tell her you called?" I actually heard him smile. "Hi Libby. It's good to hear your voice. You doing well?" Dang, he's changed. I barely remember him. Well, he used to give me and D rides to the street basketball games and he'd make sure we had food. But that's all I really remember about him. He was gone to the service for the majority of my childhood. But he's the reason why they all call me Libby. I used to go to the family gatherings they have once a week. He wasn't there when I was attending. He was stationed in Fort Campbell in Kentucky for about two years. Left there and was stationed at Fort Polk after the second tour in Iraq. "Yeah David, I've been good." I got shy all of a sudden. He was family but I didn't know his character. "Listen. There is something wrong with Doll. And it's got something to do with her love interest. I found some 'stuff' to indicate that the heifer means my sister more harm than good. I'm trying to be good. But I want to shoot her on sight." He was talking calmly but with clenched teeth. That's not a good sign.

"David, what did you find and did it smell like sulfur?" If we can come to an agreement of what is happening we might be able to handle Dahlia together. "As a matter of fact it did. I felt bad mojo when I met that girl. After all this stuff I found under Doll's bed, I want her dead. If it's alright with you, I want to have a meeting with all of y'all women folk and the Emerely boys. It's time to get my sister out of the clutches of this she-devil. I'll put down some salt here and I need for you to do the same at every entry at your house. Tell Doll she can't leave til we all talk, which might be tomorrow evening." Now I don't know nothing about no salt. That sounds like voodoo to me. I didn't say anything about it though. Seems like David knows what he's talking about. He broke through my thoughts. "Alright Fam. Love you. Holla." He hung up before I could reply. He felt like a blessing. David seemed to reinforce what God was doing. He was putting the right people in my life to make this attempt to do right be permanent. I couldn't do anything but smile and tell God "Thank ya".

I'll go ahead and round up the crew, including Adonis. I don't know why I am involving him in all this. It just seems like he should be here, even if only for my benefit. Plus I want everybody to meet him. I guess I'm acting like D was when she wanted to bring Tracie to church. She was so happy that she wanted everyone she loved and cared about to share in her happiness. I get it. I just don't want her to be happy on the surface, I want her to be happy through and through. As I went to get a box of salt to empty all over my house I began to pray. I wanted God to restore Dahlia to her health and happiness. I know it is partially my fault why she lost it. I made peace with what's happened to me. But I never thought about Dahlia peace. She lost so much that night in the fall of the year. That was the first cool night of the season. It was the night they put my mama in the ground. We couldn't have been no more than 13.

Terry J Dawkins was his name. He was my sperm donor. I didn't even know his name until two days before mama died. She told me that and so much more about him. A part of me wanted to know him. I wanted to know more about him. Seemed like if I knew about him, I'd know about me too. Mama warned me about him. Said he was the definition of a sinner and that I should stay away. I didn't listen. What little girl you know doesn't wanna know their daddy? I should've ran away when he smiled at me at the funeral and beaconed me closer so that he could hug me. I should've screamed when he hugged me so tight I thought my breast would burst. I didn't see the signs because I didn't know them. It took a while for me to not accept any blame. Now that I'm older I blame no one but Terry James Dawkins Sr.

That evening after the funeral I walked home to be alone. I needed to collect my thoughts and cry alone. My little cousin, Andrew, walked with me. He was my shadow back then. Where I went, he went. Little did we know Terry followed close behind. We got home and I went to my room to change and be alone. Next thing I know, my bedroom door flew open. "You know...you turned out to be a pretty girl. You look a lot like your mama. I was hoping you ain't act nothing like her. But chu hot in the ass just like she was around your age." The whole time he was talking he was undressing. I wanted to run, but he was blocking the door. I could hear my little cousin Andy running for me. It was like he heard my thoughts. He took off through the back door. I knew exactly where he was going. Help would be here soon. I just hoped it would be soon enough.

Truthfully, I was scared. But I was becoming angry. I wanted him to know that I knew the secrets. "You need to get out of my room. My mama told me what you did to her. She told me how I got here. I know you raped her. That's why she couldn't keep me. She hated me because of you. You ruined me. I didn't have a mama because of you. GET OUT YOU SON OF A BITCH!" I had learned that term from girls at school. My aunt would have knocked my front teeth out if she heard me cuss. I was standing there trying to catch my breath. My chest rising and falling like I had a chance in this fight. Dahlia told me that even if you can't win, you let the world know you were there. He reached for me. I dodged him and scratched him in the face. That made him mad. He laughed all wild and loud. "Son of a bitch huh? So you've got a little fire. So do I." He reached out again and smacked me across the face so hard that I hit the floor.

He picked me up by my throat and drugged me from the floor to the bed. He started ripping off my clothes. I knew I was in trouble. I kicked, punched, bit. I had to let the world know I was there. He covered my mouth. I could taste blood and sweat. So I knew I got him good. He entered inside of me. I was in so much pain. I just wanted to die. I don't know which one hurt me the most; his manhood or my inability to win this fight. He only got one thrust. The next thing I heard was Dahlia's voice. It was eerily calm. "Tell Hell Dahlia sent-chu." Then I heard a loud firecracker. I felt warm liquid spray on my face. Saw a lot of blood sling against the wall. I felt the air, the last breath, hiss out of his lungs. Terry James Dawkins Sr was dead. My daddy was dead on top of me. Dead weight has a definition that most will never truly understand. I'm a living witness, the dead is heavy. I was in shock, I couldn't move. I couldn't scream. I couldn't do anything but cry.

I heard more footsteps. I heard a man say, "What's your name darlin'?" I heard Dahlia say, "Dahlia, but that's my best friend Liberty under that man. Can you help me get her out?" Her voice was shaky and strained, like she was crying too. "Okay Dahlia, I'll help you. But only if you give me the gun, okay?" I couldn't see anything. I heard another man's voice. "DROP THE GUN AND GET DOWN ON THE FLOOR!" I heard the first man's voice say, "It's okay man. Dahlia was just about to hand me the gun anyway. We've got to get her friend from under the man so she can breathe. Right Dahlia?" I don't know what else was said. I blacked out. Next thing I knew I was at the hospital. Dahlia and most of her brothers were there. There was an officer there. But I didn't know him. The voices I'd heard earlier didn't belong to him.

Dahlia swore to me two things that night. Number one: she'd always love me and she'd always be there for me when I needed her to be. Number two: we'd learn to defend ourselves at any cost. Guns, knives, hand to hand combat; we'd become skilled fighters. So nobody could ever hurt us. It's been almost twenty years and she's kept both promises. We all can fight. All of us in our crew. We can all shoot. We all carry knives. We're all there for one another no matter what. Today is no different. Dahlia needs, we provide. As much as she's done for the rest of us. She's literally killed for me. The least I can do is be there for her now.

"Father. Thank you for second chances. Thank you for the opportunity to be a giver and not just the usual receiver. Help me to be strong. Help me to do what's necessary for my family. Please touch Dahlia with your love. She's hurting. She has run to dangerous things for the love she seeks. I know that feeling. I don't want her to feel that pain that comes afterwards. The pain of knowing that you put your own self in bad situations running away from the past. Oh God, please guide me in the right direction to help the girl who's been a sister to me all these years. In Jesus' name I pray, Amen." Between the words of the prayer and the sound of the salt pouring from the box, I was totally calm. I knew that everything was going to be just fine.

Chapter

11

<u>Chevy</u>

I honestly needs a drank! I've been doing so well. I haven't had a drink in almost 96 hours. That hasn't happened in approximately two years. I'm proud, but I'm tired of being strong. I'm just saying. I needs me a drank. I feel so aware of my surroundings. That is not polite! I want to feel numb. There is nothing wrong with numb. Numb is a virtue. Blessed are the numb for they shall be content. That should be a bible verse in drunkalations. Yes, this is what my brain is reduced to at two in the morning. I don't want to start taking sleeping pills. That's just another avenue of addiction. Not walking from one party into another. The shame in it all is that I need to talk to somebody and don't want to talk to nobody. I text Evan earlier. Even as the thought runs through my head it made me smile. That brother there is something special. I ain't afraid to admit it either. His voice makes a fire grow in places I ought to be ashamed to mention.

I've actually been a lady in our conversations. My desire to do right has a slight lead over the "ho" deep inside. That's been surprising. Since my husband, the predator, died all I've been is Mississippi's popular delicacy; a ho cake. I'm not going to make church-house promises of what I will become. I'm just saying there will be no stirring of the honey pot today. Liberty says one day at a time will get you way farther than planning ahead.

Speaking of Lib, she's acting differently. She's so calm. Usually my girl is so dramatic! But for the past day or so, she's been a cucumber; cool and refreshing. She called earlier and said that we all need to meet up at her house. I told her if she cooks, I'm there. I've been eating out a lot the past few days. I'm sick of it. She told me she'd cook a big pot of spaghetti with meatballs and cheese toast. I got so excited! I told her I'd bring the cheesecake, sprite and Hawaiian punch. She asked me if I was okay. I told her that I just haven't had a home cooked meal in a while. She said, "You didn't mention the Tito's vodka that usually accompanies this punch." I told her that I'm trying to do better. "Well I'm proud. If you need me, text me." That's not like her. I mean, she can be supportive and things. But she meant it. Usually Lib is selfish. If it's self-serving, she's all for it. But if it's' totally selfless...she says the right words but the feeling is way over there somewhere. I honestly felt like I could count on her. Now I'll be honest. I don't expect this to last long, but I'm going to enjoy it and milk it while it's here.

No matter how hard I try not to, my mind keeps drifting back to Michelle and Adrian. She's such a sweet girl. And Adrian is an old fashion southern gentleman. After he got his box of his father's belongings, he begged his mom to drop him off at the house so he could thank me personally and maybe do some heavy lifting around the house. She told me he said, "Since there's no man around to help her, that's the least I can do. I mean, she gave me a piece of my dad." When he came to the door, I had to shake the shock from my face. He looks identical to the man I fell in love with. Feature wise, he is Nathan Devonte' "Dade" Davidson at age 16. It's like Michelle was just the incubator and nothing else. But his character is totally Michelle. He's gentle and sweet, caring and strong, rather mannish but polite. She is doing a great job raising him. She needs to hold a conference with the other side chicks who have birthed the seeds of chucky.

One of the younger boys, Trenton McMiller, is full of the devil. I tell no stories. This beautifully chocolate five year old image of my husband actually slapped me on the behind, turned around and said, "Ma look, I made dat ass jiggle." Before I knew it, I had snatched him up by the collar and threatened his life. His mother stepped to me and said, "I will beat cho ass bout my son." I told her, "First, you oughta try beating your son's ass. There is the box of Dade's stuff. Get it and yo sex offender in training and get out." She saw this as the opportunity to step to me, but the look of warning on my face persuaded her to do as directed. She grabbed the box and told her kid to follow her out the door. He looked back and winked his eye and smiled at me just like his father used to. Like what is she doing? Is she not raising him at all? But he's got his father's blood. Some bad behavior is inherited. If I had to place a bet. Trenton Dade

McMiller will have been arrested at least twice by his 17th birthday behind money and some woman.

I really didn't want any part of those children's lives. But I'll deal with Adrian. And to be honest, I was thinking that would've been partial. However, I don't feel it's my responsibility to be there for any of the women my husband cheated with. But I felt like Michelle was somehow my fault. She was just a child when my nasty husband hunted her all because I had a faulty uterus. That and her personality is wonderful. She has sense. She has class. She's actually raising her son as opposed to just keeping him. And for the record, there is a difference. If you see your kid as your equal and they don't fear you in any way, they have the ability to talk back and verbally question your decisions; you're keeping them. If your children have a set schedule, chores, expectations, and they are too scared to try you; you're raising them. These young mama's out here trying to be their child's friend. You better make damn sure you can handle that set up. Friends fight. Friends keep secrets from each other. Friends will leave you high and dry if you decide not to take their advice. A friend will take your man. Friends will embarrass you in public when they don't get their way. If that's what you want from your child, then let it be. But if not you better get it together and start to raise, teach, instill values, and discipline your child. I'm almost glad I have no children. I don't have the stomach for it. I'll kill a kid. My mouth is flip because my patience is thin. If I tell you once you better get it. I don't repeat myself. My friends know that. My coworkers have learned it.

My last sexual encounter had to learn it the hard way. I told him my normal goodbye bit. "Well dude, it's been real and it's been fun. It's even been real fun. But all good things must come to an end. Don't call me no more player." He grabbed me by my arm and pulled me back. "Whatchu mean?" I smiled at him and walked away. I guess he thought he was going to change my mind. I had flowers waiting for me at the office the next morning. I politely put them on my secretary's desk. She laughed. "Ya done broke another heart Ms. Chevy?" I just laughed at her and walked back to my office. Apparently he was watching the whole exchange. He came to my office. "So you gone just give my flowers away? Girl you don't know me do you?" He decided to knuck by reaching over my desk and grabbing me by my collar. So I bucked by putting my Desert Eagle

357 to his temple and cocking it. My secretary, Tisha, opened the door to my office with her own gun drawn.

"Lu lu lu look baby, I'm out. I just want you for myself. That's that's that's all." You know when you've evoked fear when a grown man eyes well with tears and he begins to stutter. It tickled me. Why is it when a pitiful excuse of a man gets upset with a woman, who doesn't even belong to him, he thinks he can use violence and persuade her into submission? Do you honestly think a real black woman is going to put up with that and not get you back? Pitiful soul. I scared him to death with a smile on my face. He let me go. I lowered my weapon and so did Tisha. He walked out. Tisha looked at me and said in her Cajun tongue, "Ya know he pissed dem pants, right?" She was laughing before I could respond.

"You so wrong...that man was scared for his life Tish." I was laughing too. You better know what you're grabbing on a woman like that. "Gurl, he high on stupidity. Ya must 'ave made him feel like a man. A real man. Ya betta quit leevin' dis trail of brok-un hearts. Or you'll have to get a record." I looked at her with a puzzle piece etched in my forehead. "A criminal record Cherie." I shook my head. I knew she was right. I needed to be more responsible with my "night life". And since that day months ago, I have been much better. I guess I've been changing and didn't realize it til now.

My phone just looks so enticing. Let me call my mama. It's been quite a while since we've talked. I grabbed the phone and noticed the time; it's 4:22 in the morning. It's too early to call anybody and yet against the permission of my mind I unlock the screen and find my mama's place in contacts. The phone rings...once...twice..."Chevy? Baby? What's the matter?" Now she didn't bit mo sound as if I woke her up.

"Evelyn Marie Washington! Why you woke?" I laughed at her. She's a mama to the bone. Then again, I am calling her mighty early. "I'm fine mama. I just couldn't sleep. So I wanted to hear your voice. It's been a while, you know?" She laughed at me. "Oh lawd child! You miss your mama? Get that way sometime. I'm grown with grandchil'luns and I go to the home to see mine at least twice a week. But I've been up with arthritis pain shooting through this knee. It's gonna rain soon, I know that!" She paused and grunted. I'm sure she was rubbing that knee and massaging it with her thumb.

"My knee has been bothering me ever since your baby sister decided that I was too young to die. That's what the gal said too. 'Mama I want you to be around a long time. You've got to get in shape. We going to eat clean and work out, okay?' I been walking at least two miles every day with that little girl. Now what's eating at your conscious keeping you up?" I wanted to hear more about what all Marissa was making mama do to keep her young. "Well mama, nothing. I'm having a hard time sleeping tonight. I wanna hear more about You eating clean." I laughed. We southern. Eating clean ain't exactly in our makeup. We eat a lot of vegetables as long as they've been seasoned with fat back, salt meat, smoked neck bone, or hog maul.

"Child I'm so sick of a salad! If I got to eat one more this week somebody is gone get it!" I hollered. My mama had me rolling at 4:30 in the morning. I had to sit up for this conversation. Mama is a little stocky. But 8 kids will do that to you. She still has a pretty shape as long as she wears a bra. But she has tickled me about these salads. I hear her laughing at me laughing at her. "I tell you the truth. Taco salad, grilled chicken salad, tuna salad, fried chicken salad, fruit salad, pulled pork salad; I'm right ready to give it up! I would shoot somebody for a fried pork chop sandwich, French fries with plenty of salt, and a twenty ounce coke cola. Do you hear me?! Help me hold out Jesus!"

I'm just a laughing while she's telling me about her issues with "eating right". "The problem is, it's working. Girl I done lost about 10 pounds fooling around with Marissa. I told her what she's doing is working. Don't tell her about me grumbling and complaining. I've been doing rather well sticking to her plan. Although I will admit, I'll sneak and get me some of them M&Ms every other day. Just the fun size bag of the peanut kind. A little sugar won't hurt anything. I don't think.

"Mama, you sneaking and eating wrong?" I knew that would get her started again. "Child that's my money. Marissa ain't got job the first. I appreciate her helping me 'not die' as she so nicely put it. But if I want some sugar, that's my right. I ain't gone go overboard." She got quiet. "Mama?" She clears her throat. "I'm here baby. I just got to thinking. We do God the same way I'm doing Marissa. We tell God we'll do better and sometimes we actually follow through, like I'm doing with eating clean. But then we have a power struggle and go and do something that will set us back a step or two trying to show God whose boss. Like we've got sense...and ain't. Let me put them M&Ms in the garbage." I heard her grunt as she got out of the chair. She had a point. Never thought of it that way. But that is typical of me. I will keep this conversation in mind as I "keep on keeping on" with my sobriety.

"Mama, I've got some things to finish up here and then I'm taking a vacation; a two week vacation. I wanna come home for a week and see the whole family. The next week, I want you to go away with me for a few days. You think that'll be alright?" I really missed my family. They are scattered about. We text or email each other maybe once a week. Some of us once a month. Talking to mama made me miss everybody. Our conversations made me miss the complex-less-ness of life. The calmness of living is the way my life used to be before I met Dade. It's time for me to return back to that concept of life.

"Yeah baby! That sounds mighty fine to me. Now you got to wait till I can get into this dress I like. I done bought it a size too small. They say it's a good way to encourage yourself to lose weight. If I don't lose the weight, I'll put on one of them girdles that suck everything in from your ribs to your knees. I see'd one of them on Instagram. That girl had love handles, a gut and flabby thighs. But when she put that long girdle on she looked like somebody in that dress. Sho nuff did! Hey hey hey! I'm gone get me one a dem dere." I started back laughing at my mama trying to be young with a pair of spanx. I guess I know what I'll be getting her for her birthday.

"Mama, I'll call you with more details about a vacation for the two of us. You can help pick out the destination and the date. I'm about to get off this phone with you and get my day started. You got my side hurting laughing at you and a 'long girdle'. I hope you have a great day. I love you mama." She was laughing at me. "I loves you too, Chevy. I'll be looking forward to that call, young lady." And with that she hung up. She doesn't believe in saying goodbye. She says that goodbye is too final. She only says that to people she's dismissing from her life. If she loves you, she'll just disconnect the call. That's something I need to do. I need to tell Dade and my life with him goodbye. I need to terminate these emotions and that will help me dismiss this overindulgence in alcohol. A conversation with mama is just what I needed.

Chapter

12

<u>Byrd</u>

"But Lib, what's really going on?" I was trying to get as much information out of Liberty as I could. I was also stalling. I needed to make sure I had the sign I had been praying for. I begged God for a sign as to when I'm to "spill the tea" if you will. I don't want to be fast and do more harm than good. "Byrd, um…there are some forces at work to destroy Dee. One thing I know for sure is that it won't work. If we all come together and do whatever needs to be done, we can put this thing to rest." I breathe in deeply and ask a simple question that deserves a simple answer. But that answer holds a whole lot of meaning. "Lib, is Tracey going to be there?" I heard a laugh. Not a belly laugh. But an attitude was trapped in her throat. "I wish she would show up at my door. I will gladly send her on to hell with a smile. But moving on, be here at 3:00." Okay, that's all I really needed to know. I've got some explaining to do. "Yes ma'am Mother Hubbard." I heard her smile. "Bye crazy."

I disconnected the call and looked my new boo, Nigel, in the face. "You've got plans for 3 o'clock?" He looked at me with confusion. "Will I be next to you?" I smiled nervously. "Uh yes sir. But you'll be looking Dahlia Emerely in the face along with the rest of us." He looked down at his hands for a few seconds. I just paused and waited for him to look back up at me so I could tell him he didn't have to go home but he had to hop the hell up out of my house. I don't need no weakling backing me up for this fight. This is my family. I'll always pull out the big guns and an even bigger attitude for mi familia. But when he looked back up at me he had the biggest smile plastered across his face with tears rolling down those smooth and high cheeks. I was honestly baffled.

"I'd be happy to go with you. Thank you for asking." Now it was my turn to be confused. "Why are you crying dude? What did I say?" He got up and walked towards me. He put his hands on my face. "Korede, you have answered my prayers. I begged God for the chance to make it right. You're presenting me with that opportunity. Thank you so much. You could've ran the other way when I approached you. When I told you the whole truth about who I am and what I was, you listened to the voice of the Lord instead of feeling threatened and afraid. Thank you. Looking at you is...it's like staring mercy right in the face. I know it is way too early in our relationship to say this. But I love you. You are a beautiful person inside and out. And when God gets through with you, you'll be a living breathing example of the scripture, 'God has not given us the spirit of fear, but of power, and of love, and of a sound mind."

Now the whole time he's talking there is a feeling settling around me that I've only felt in church. It is all calming, energizing and all consuming. It felt right. I allowed the words he spoke to tear down the wall that I had up around my heart. I didn't say a word because I wanted God to do what he wanted to without my opinion or input. I just let the tears flow as the bricks fell. "Korede'. This has been the quickest romance that I've ever been a part of. It usually takes me months to feel interested in a woman. I'm always a gentleman. But to really be into a lady, it takes me some time. It had to have been the hand of God on this. I feel like I've known you for years and it only took two days. No matter what, please know I'll always be in your corner looking out for you." And with that he kissed me.

Now let me tell you 'bout this chea kiss! His lips shocked mine. I felt like I'd been electrocuted. That kiss brought some things to life inside my heart, my soul and of course my body. My belief became instantly restored in the race of man. Perhaps there are some knights in blue jeans out here. He conjured up some strength and confidence because when he bit my bottom lip it soared through my entire being. The passion inside of his hands felt like fire when his thumbs slid down the sides of my neck and eased the tension in my shoulders. The only thing I could do was hold on to his elbows. I was afraid if I let go I'd lose my balance. As he held me tight around my waist I could hear the wind outside and smell the scent of lavender and coconut; things I couldn't do before this encounter. The mere touch of him has heightened my senses. Who knew that all of this could happen from a kiss? Avery Sunshine knew it. As if on cue she started singing "Like This" on the radio. Nigel hummed along. And boy could he hum! It takes special skill to hum and kiss at the same time. When the time came for a break I noticed a speckle of gold in his eyes. They were mesmerizing. I literally got lost in them for a moment.

"Korede'?" I know I heard him call my name. But I couldn't move. I couldn't respond. It took his touch on my face for me to snap out of it. "Baby? You alright? Was that too soon?" I smiled and put my ear to his heart to make sure he was real. It was beating just fine. I pulled away from him and looked him in the eyes. "No. It wasn't too soon. I needed you in my life. I didn't know it. I thought I was happy and that I had everything that I needed. You came along and dropped a frightening word at the bar. It was true. I understand it now. **'You'll get what you want, but it won't be enough to keep you satisfied'.** I had all these plans of my own. It didn't necessarily include God's will for my life. I wanted Him to bless what I was going to do. I wasn't willing to die to my will for his will. So what you said was right. I hope His will is you. Nigel, I'm not sure what all you've done in your life before today. But just know that you allowed God to use you to breathe life into me. But you should've warned me! You could've said 'clear' before you shocked me like that!" He was laughing through tears. "Good God man! I'll make sure my insurance is current before I kiss you again. Even my toes feel funny." He threw his head back and hollered a country laugh that made his chest vibrate.

"Okay Ms. Byrd. I'll say clear next time I promise. But I need to go to my hotel room and mentally prepare myself for this meeting. I also need to take a shower. Something about getting clean will prepare you for anything you face. So, I'm going to leave you to your own thoughts. I encourage you to get yourself ready for 3 o'clock. I'll be here to ride with you around 2, if that's alright." He was searching my face for some clue of what all was going on in my brain. "2 will be just fine." I hugged him before he left.

A part of me wanted him to stay. Part of me wanted to tell him that we could skip the meeting with Liberty and 'nem. He was right to leave me with my thoughts. I am struggling with the tug of war inside of me. I'm already dealing with the feelings that I have about this beautiful man who has come into my life and in less than 48 hours shifted my whole perspective about life, love, and the will of God. When I look at Nigel my ideals and emotions scramble like eggs. It's as if it's impossible to depend on my own strength when

I'm around him. He makes me want to scream because of the way he unsettles me. And at the same time he's all I can think about.

If I'm going to be able to do what needs to be done to help Dahlia I need to get myself together. I'm glad that everybody is getting together to help. It's usually hard to round up the whole clan. Lib said that Dahlia's brothers will be present as well as us girls. I'm excited to see them and nervous to introduce Nigel and share his information with them. D's brothers treat us girls as though we belong to them; hella protective. But the one thing I'm going to do is apologize to D. I've been so into my own life and so into my own thing that I haven't helped much to take good care of the one that has taken good care of me.

Family is all you have. Yes, you have a life. But sometimes you have to realize and protect the people that make up that life and the sacrifices that they've made; FOR YOU. I've failed in that area for the last few months. Since my biological parents died in a car wreck years ago I've been selfish with my attention and ambition driven intentions. I've let all my girls down. They're all I've got as far as family is concerned. I dropped the ball but I refused to allow it to roll downhill. It's not just Nigel, I need to right a few wrongs of my own. This is a come to Jesus meeting for us all. Not just Dahlia.

Chapter

13

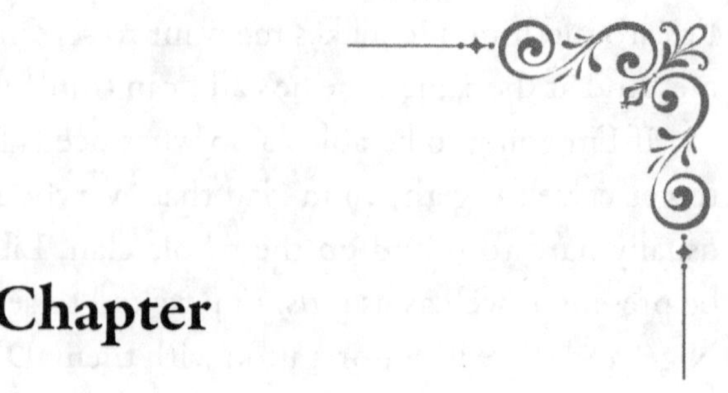

<u>Nigel</u>

After I kissed Korede' I had to get away from people, specifically her, to collect my thoughts. I have never felt this way about any lady. Never. Ever! I needed some time to fix my feelings; time to relax these emotions. So much is happening so fast. I need a moment to catch up.

That Kamden Korede' Byrd has changed my life! It's so much about her that I was looking for and had no idea I was looking. She's tough. Her exterior will run off any ill intentions. She's got a little music in her walk, but not a lot. She's extremely guarded. I like that. She's not weak and needy. She's self-sufficient. I can expect her to bring to the table and not just eat of my goods. She's smart, loving, funny, and country. She is barefoot most of the time. I love that. Be who you are with no reservations or apologies. As soon as she invited me into her house, she kicked off those shoes. I laughed because those toes of hers were so cute. Painted hot pink with white polka dots. She looked at me like she was ready to fight. "What?" I had to reign it in. "Babygirl those are the cutest toes I've ever seen and I've got 6 nieces all under the age of 10." Her face softened and she blushed. I saw a side of her that she probably tries to keep hidden. She's a little girl who misses her family.

I heard about the wreck that claimed both of her parents. I read it in the paper. I get a lot of papers delivered to me in New Orleans. I did a lot of "work" for a lot of people in a lot of different places. Getting their local paper is my way of keeping tabs on things. It was a horrible situation. Tired driver in an 18 wheeler trying to make it home for his little girl's 8th birthday. Korede's parents went for an early morning date for coffee and a walk in the park; something that was done every Wednesday morning if the weather permitted for the last 8 years or so. Korede' was getting ready for school, she was a freshman, said the Columbian Progress. Instead of boarding the bus, she was greeted by a cop car. He told her that the 18 wheeler lost control and it was nothing anyone could do, her mom and dad were killed on impact. I know the story from reading the paper. But to see its effect in her eyes, her tone, her walk; it's something to behold. She has allowed this tragedy to shape her into a wonderful, strong, beautiful woman who has no idea what it is to be loved beyond teenage angst. I followed the paper. She went on to get her GED in the summer before her Junior year. She's been arrested twice for simple assault. She was accepted into Alcorn due to her academic performance as well as her basketball skills. She dropped the ball and picked up bartending. That's where our story begins. So I guess God had been preparing me for this moment for a long time. I wasn't paying attention. Doesn't say much for me being a soothsayer now does it?

As far as soothsaying goes; God is good! He is so good. I begged and pleaded for Him to give me a chance to right my wrongs. I cried out for redemption for months and he decided to answer my plea. All the wrong, and there is so much wrong, that I've done He's forgiven. But I couldn't forgive it all. There are a few things that no matter what I cannot change. But he granted me this one opportunity and I will do whatever's necessary to clear my conscience. On top of the chance at mental salvation, I get the girl. Korede is a prize to search after. A diamond worth working for. Her outside is gorgeous with curves, dimples, and beauty marks wrapped up in flawless, caramel, well moisturized skin. But it doesn't hold a candle to the beauty, radiance, love and intelligence within. This girl is fire and ice in the same glance. I swear I wasn't looking for anybody to love. Honestly I wasn't looking for anybody at all. Korede's presence and aura slapped me in my face and made me want her more than I wanted to eat and that's my very favorite pastime. She may not know it yet, but she's my wife. We may break up. She may need the space to find out what she wants from life. But in the end, she was made for me. And I was made for her. I heard it when she got worked up at the Coup-De-Ville. I needed to care for her. She needed me to show my care. At that moment I knew that this will always be.

I come from a humongous family. We're not exactly tight knit. We love each other and we have a barbeque get-together that makes other families jealous. I want Korede a part of that type of living. She's missed out on it. I want to gift that to her. There's nothing like the electric slide with cousins and cook-offs with siblings. Nothing like hearing the laughter of a niece or a nephew. I'm ready for her to feel the warmth of the hugs from the elders of my family.

After meeting up with Korede' for the showdown of a lifetime, I became more nervous than grateful. What if I mess this up? What if I say the wrong thing? What if they don't believe me? She took one look at me and said the words I needed to hear. "Nigel, you've come too far to allow your nerves to get the best of you. You are way too smart to ask God for something that you can't handle. And God is way too good to give you a task that you can't complete. Get it together." With that she kissed me on my cheek, rubbed my back and gave me the strength I needed to shut my thoughts down. That was confirmation of what my heart has discovered; she's the one for me. I smiled at her and she had a twinkle in her eye that wasn't there before. It was a knowing that registered in her soul. I'm not sure what it was, but I liked it and I plan to investigate further. While you're in Korede's presence, you don't have the sinister demon of doubt plaguing you. She brings clarity and peace to the table. That is a luxury very few people get to experience. While riding over to Liberty's house, I kept stealing glances at Korede'. There was a rush of heat and cool that plagued my senses and invaded my skin and without my consent I began to pray aloud the words I heard in my head.

"Father, if it be your will, let this man be the man for me in this season that I'm in. Allow him to build me up and not tear me down. Let him see the You in my character and not try to change who I am to fit his own agenda. God do your thing in me and him. I'll give you all the praise and glory. In Jesus' name...Amen." She looked at me with her mouth wide open in disbelief. She pulled into a vacant parking lot, slammed the car in park and took off her seatbelt. She faced me with tears in her wide eyes and a mix of wonder and uncertainty etched in her forehead. "Nigel? How did you know...where did you hear those words? What kind of man are you?" Her questions were warranted but her tears were not. She started shivering like she was cold.

"Korede'? Why are you crying? And what do those words mean to you?" I wiped her tears away with my thumbs. Then swept over me a mixture of relief, hurt, acceptance and joy. She couldn't speak and for the life of me I couldn't stop. "Korede'? I'm just going to start talking. I'm going to tell you everything I hear. Don't be alarmed or ashamed, okay?" She just nodded her head. I think she was afraid to trust her mouth to speak. I understand because I've been there many, many times. I closed my eyes and concentrated on the feelings that had warmed and cooled my skin. "I hear you when you talk to me in this car. I appreciate the fact that you keep the passenger seat clean so that I can feel comfortable. I love our talks. It gives me great joy to share in every part of your life. You've learned what the cold chills are for. You're catching on quickly. Never forget about them. You were dealt a tough hand. You've handled it with grace and I am so proud of you. The angels watch over you and report to me your progress. Heaven smiles on you and your tenacity to live in spite of life. I want you to know I love you. Kamdyn I love you so much! Yes I was laughing at you. And to answer your question. Yes, you can have him."

When I opened my eyes to look into hers, they were closed. Her tears were flowing freely yet there was a smile on her face. She still shivered. She opened her eyes and looked directly into mine. "Thank you Nigel. I needed that in ways that I can't explain. You've got to be the best thing for me because I've never cried in front of any man and I've known you less than 48 hours and you've seen me cry twice." She laughed and wiped her face with her hands. She looked at her hands covered in her tears. She laughed again. "It looks like we're going to be late getting to Lib's house. I've got to go back home and fix my face." I had to laugh at her, because I understood. She's seen me cry too! I've got siblings who haven't seen me cry yet. She turned the car around and headed back to her place.

Once we were actually headed to the gathering, I was paying close attention to how I felt. The closer we got, the stronger my gift was and the more my senses heightened. I was aware of every demon in the woods and every ghost in the cemeteries that we passed. In New Orleans the final resting places are above ground and the feeling is normal, I guess, when you pass by. But in Mississippi where the ground is solid, the dead rest there in. It seems like in theory there shouldn't be much of a difference between in the ground or on top of it as long as you're dead, but there is. The churches house most of the dead here, and there's a church at every corner. The vibes you get from riding around this town can spook you, if you let it. I'm on a mission. I've got a job to do and I will do it well. As the old people would say "I've got a soul to fit for the sky."

I refuse to allow the ghosts of Mississippi stop me from giving this God given chance all I've got. I was so lost in thought that I didn't pay close attention to how to get to Liberty's house. Once we arrived I couldn't help noticing the shell casings on the ground. I was so overcome with the feeling of laughter that I had to somehow try to hide. Liberty ain't no punk! I loved her already. These ladies are a handful! And the men that love them will have to learn when to let them be and when to step up their game and be the men they need to lead.

Once inside, Korede' announced that I was here and I was the new boo. I got nods and smiles and side eyes. She made her way around the room giving hugs and fist bumps to those same smiles and side eyes. David came and sat beside me. He said his hello's, how you doing's and where you from's. He looked at me dead in my face and said I thought you looked familiar. I was at a revival meeting one night and you were there. I prayed for you. I'm glad you're alright. My eyes widened. That was the night that I gave my soul to God for him to save it. I was close to losing my way for good. I knew it too. That's the difference between me and a lot other people. There comes a time when you have to admit that you are at the end of your rope. Some people try to act like they aren't afraid, or they don't know how bad things have gotten. Never lie to yourself. Be aware of who you are and what you are doing. Pay attention to the shape you're in as well as how deep the rabbit hole goes. You know when you've left safe territory. And I knew I was way off course that night. I had been into some things that I had lost control over; they were now controlling me. I had no God on my side. I needed Him back.

"Yeah, I was there. I heard God say, you'd be fine. I'm glad I got to see it for myself. I'm glad you're good man." That gave me the confidence I needed to do all I had to do. I realized that God was setting me up from the jump. Not only did I just meet my wife. But I just met my brother too. This is more than I could've asked for. "Well David, I appreciate you praying for me. I was in a very bad place. It was either God or grave at that point." He just nodded his head as if he totally understood. "Nigel, step outside and talk to me about something." I followed him out the front door as this clean cut brother was getting out of his car.

He was muscular, clean shaven and walked like army. Which had nothing on his character. Just because of who I am, I can tell a lot about you by the way you walk. This dude had power. I'm talking about Holy Ghost power. Man...I wanted to start crying. All he did was walk toward me. Once he was on the porch, he shook hands with David. "You must be Dahlia's brother. I'm Adonis. It's good to meetchu." I looked at David and he looked like he was about to cry. I had to clear my throat and swallow that emotion or I was going to sound like a 14 year old boy who was just starting to change his tone.

David looked to me for help. I couldn't let him down. I held out my hand and introduced myself. "I'm Nigel. I'm with Korede." He looked at David with confusion in his eyes. David said. "He's with Byrd. The youngest of them all." Adonis nodded his head in understanding. David spoke again. "Adonis, I want to talk to the two of you away from my brothers, if that's alright." Adonis nodded his head and said, "Let me put down the paper dinnerware and grab a cup of coffee. I'll be right back."

I started putting two and two together. Clean shaven black man, army posture, and coffee in the middle of the day...this man is police! Plus he wasn't too bothered by the shell casings which meant he knew where they had come from. So this is Liberty's man. I bet that's how they met; over shell casings. What a romance!? David looked at me and said, "Did you feel that?" I smiled at him. "You mean that lay you out anointing that's on Adonis?" David nodded his head. I laughed and said, "Maaaan I was close to lifting my hands to receive it." David laughed with me. He dried his eyes because he really was about to cry while meeting Adonis. All I could do was shake my head.

I know everyone has to work out their own soul's salvation. But spiritually, I wanted to be like him when I grew up! He was the embodiment of the scripture, "Behold, I give unto you power to tread upon serpents and scorpions and over all the power of the enemy; nothing shall by any means hurt you". The way he carried himself; he just looked like there should be a bible book named after him. Aside from the reason I'm here with the work that I have to do, I'm so glad I came! I'm being linked together with a band of brothers with power and pull. That's so important to me because I begged God to not let me be alone in this walk of right. I begged him to place the right people in my life to help me be better than I can on my own. And He's doing just that.

Adonis walked back out with coffee in his hand and a smile on his face. "What's going on, y'all?"

Chapter

14

<u>Adonis</u>

When I got out of my car there were two men on Liberty's porch. One looked a lot like Dahlia and the other not at all. When we all gave a proper introduction, for some strange reason they were a little too quiet for me; apprehensive almost. It's as if they have something to hide. Between my investigative skills and the spirit of discernment, I'd figure it out soon enough. I walked in to give Liberty what she'd asked for, napkins, paper plates and cups. She had a smile on her face that made my heart warm. I've never seen her smile that big and that sincere. I love that. I hope that God grants me the opportunity to keep that smile on her face for the rest of my life. She told me thank you, by handing me a cup of coffee. By the smell alone I could tell this was Community brand coffee which is my favorite. I like the fancy stuff well enough. But give me Community coffee with half and half and sugar any day.

I sipped my coffee and smiled at her back. There was an ease to what was going on between us. I absolutely love every minute of it. She was taking care of me and I was taking care of her. And it came naturally; nothing forced like the beginning of most relationships. This was my kind of woman, and I knew I was her kind of man. I was briefly introduced to the young gentlemen sitting in front of the ball game, Ms. Kamdyn Korede' Byrd. I received hellos and handshakes from all of them. Byrd is cute yet troubled. And by my interactions with Liberty I assumed she was dangerous as well. I think all of these women are. I believe they are all trained to protect themselves at all costs. But none of them seem to know how to take care of themselves. They are not well rounded individuals. That's why God made them a help mate. Liberty called me aside and asked if I'd seen David and Byrd's new boo. I told her they are on the porch and I'm going out to speak with them now. She stated that David has a lot more information about the reason why we are gathered here today. In other words she was suggesting that I go and get the goods. "I got you baby." I winked at her and left out the front door.

Once I got out on the porch, David was smiling and wiping his eyes. Nigel was laughing. The good hearted nature of these two was now plain to see. First impressions can be deceiving. But I still feel like there's something being hidden and I wanted in. Nigel looked at me with hope in his eyes. "Adonis, don't get offended; please. But you've got so much God in you and so much power on you that you are hard to take in all at once. I wanna just tell you that before we go any further. We were trying not to cry, rock and hum when you walked up here. I mean...Dude! Where did you come from?" I had to laugh. I've heard that a few times before. I thought it was the cop cologne. That's what they call the police presence. But I didn't realize that my relationship with God was strong enough to be seen by people without the subject of Him being the topic of our conversation. That explains why they were polite and slightly cold a few moments ago. They were trying to keep their composure. My grandfather had that air about him as well. You knew who he served before he opened his mouth. Of course to me he was just grandpa and I never knew what all the fuss was about. "Well I'm sorry fellas."

David held up his hand and stopped me from speaking. "Never apologize about that. Now a warning would have been nice." We all got tickled. "But an apology is never necessary." We all shook hands and I felt so much better. David patted me on my back and said, "We need to talk. We all have some introductions to make; some situations to explain. Some requests to make. I think I'd like to start."

We sat in the rockers like the old timers used to do when I was a kid. It just felt right. It felt like home. I like that. David opened his mouth and I could literally see the pain and concern etched in his face. "Dahlia is my sister. The only one I know about." He laughed. "Hey...Papa was a rolling stone." He cleared his throat because he's clearly getting emotional. "She's in spiritual and physical danger. She's a lesbian who's opened the door to her heart and home for a young lady who seeks to cause her harm. This young lady has a strong and deep root on my sister. I can't tell you why because I don't know what the cause of it is. I just know I'm too weak to lift it. So let me just put it out there, I know and practice white and gray magick and this..." He stopped to get his emotions under control. He continued again, but in a shaky voice. "This here is beyond me. I need as much help as I can get. I'm begging for the both of you to help in any way that you can."

The church has taught me and the Bible says to flee the very appearance of evil. Everything in me wanted to get up and walk off. I have never met anyone who's ever admitted to me that they deal in witchcraft. But I heard the Spirit of the Lord clear as a bell say with finality, "Don't. You. Move. I've placed you here, amongst your brethren." So I did exactly what he said. I nodded my head and allowed them to continue talking. Nigel said, "Well I'm just going to come out and say it. That young lady you speak of paid me to put the root on your sister. I didn't know Dahlia...still don't. But I did know what I got paid to do. I'm here to lift if off of her. See, I gave my soul to a God who forgives, but I couldn't seem to. I begged God to allow me at least one do over. At least one chance to get it right. I started studying the profile pictures on social media of some of the people I've had to do work for and on. I saw Dahlia and all these beautiful women. I burned the faces of each woman in my brain. I said if I ever saw one, I'd take the chance to clear my conscience. I met Byrd a few nights ago at the college bar where she works. I was getting my nephew settled in and I went to blow off some steam. I got a drink and recognized her face from the pictures. I whispered some words of advice in her ear to get her attention, with all intents and purposes of getting here to undo what I have done. I'm skilled in white, gray, and black magick. I've done it for years; since I was 6 years old. The burden of this curse is not a problem for me to lift. The only problem is the shame I feel that I'm causing someone else pain. That hinders me from doing all I can in the strength that I am. I'm going to need some help."

The look on my face had to have been priceless. I was totally shocked. I didn't know what to say. But most importantly I wondered if I was going to have to break up a fight on this porch. If some man had said that he'd put a harmful thing on my sister, I'd probably be livid and ready to kill him. I started praying and asking God to remove whatever tension was on this porch. But then I stopped because I honestly didn't feel any tension. I heard the Spirit of the Lord again, "Watch me work."

David looked at Nigel "Man...you got me! I was shocked at the words you said. The truth of what you said hit me like a ton of bricks. But, I totally understand what you're saying. You did what you were paid to do. I mean I've done it. Not exactly to your extent, because I didn't have the power or the know-how. If you came here to right a wrong, I'm going to help you as much as I can. Most importantly you've come to help my sister. As far as I'm concerned you're just like one of those nappy headed boys in that living room looking at the game. You're my brother and I appreciate you so much."

He shook his hand and patted him on the back. I was blown away seeing Grace at work. Forgiveness is an amazing thing. The more I thought about all that Nigel confessed the more I understood why I needed to be here. They both looked at me. And with a grateful heart I silently asked God for the words to say. "Well, I'm just a cop. I'm a god fearing man. I know more about spiritual warfare than I'd care to admit, although I believe y'all know way more about it than me. Honestly, I'm brand new to what you've said your skills and experiences are. I had a mind to run off the porch and leave you two where you sat. But God told me not to move. Now, after hearing the both of you out, I feel like I've known the two of you for years. God introduced me to my wife and she turned around and introduced me to my brothers. I only have knowledge of the God that I've been raised to serve to offer. But I do offer to you the Him in me. I'd be glad to do whatever I can."

Nigel let out a breath of air and tears fell from his eyes and disappeared in his beard. I looked at him with a question in my eyes. He said, "The God in you is more than either of us could handle. Maannnn, you just don't know how big and richly God dwells in you. I can see light coming out of your mouth when you talk. That's no small feat. Believe me when I tell you, you've got plenty to offer. I wanna be like you when I grow up." My mouth flew open in shock. I looked at David. He had his eyes closed with tears flowing down his face as well, mumbling something I couldn't hear. "Don't get me wrong, I know God. I hear Him when he speaks. I can see Him when he moves. But the power you possess allows people to understand God and the seriousness of His kingdom when you walk. You're an enforcer of Heavenly principals who just happens to also enforce the law of the land. So trust me, you have just as much or more to offer in this fight than you think. This fight affects you too." Nigel took a deep breath and started giving me the history and foundation of the sisterhood between these four women. "It all started with Liberty. See, Liberty's father was also a rolling stone. He had a daughter a year before Liberty name Na'treiel Latice Gifford. The woman we know as Tracy, aka 'Dahlia's girlfriend.'" I had to stop him right there. I needed to breathe. So this Tracy lady is coming after Dahlia and Liberty. But Liberty has no idea that this is her half-sister! If she knew, she'd have told me. This does affect me. This demon is coming against my future.

With emotion in my chest that wasn't there before, I started talking. "Um...hold it. We need to pray." David popped his eyes open and looked at me like a man on his last leg. "I thought you'd never say that. What took you so long?" He smiled at me. We all leaned forward in the rockers. I started talking..."God I call you my father and you call me your son. I need you to guide me. I need you to lead me. I know that you've been working fast these last few days. I can feel bonds and ties to people I honestly don't know. But I know that you did it. There is no logical way that you would put us together just to suffer the heartache of loss. I'm begging you to lead us and guide us in the right directions. We all have a skill and a talent that can be used for the building of your kingdom. This day is a day of change. It is the day we tear Satan's kingdom down. He means to destroy. You've brought us together to defend. We are willing and we are ready. Let our coming together not be in vain. I trust you and love you more than I need to inhale oxygen. And I have learned that obedience makes you happy. I'm ready to make you happy. Just tell me what to do. In Jesus' Name, Amen."

They all said Amen. Nigel looked at David and said, "Your gift is getting stronger by the minute." David looked at Nigel and said, "I'll do anything for family." I looked at David and said "What does that mean?" David grinned like the cat looking at the canary. "I said a few chants and drank a potion earlier to boost what and who I am to save my sister. Nothing sinister. Nothing permanent. Just what was necessary. Nothing to worry about." I looked at David and wondered, what did he drink? Then I started to expect an answer from the Lord. He's usually never far off with requested instructions. Nigel got ready to tell the rest of what he knows. "Tracy knows that Dahlia is the one who killed her father, but she doesn't know why. And..." He stopped talking.

I started looking around to see if I could see what he saw. I saw nothing. I waved my hand in front of his face to see if he'd come out of the trance he was in. I softly called his name so that I wouldn't alarm the people in the house. David held his finger up to his lips to indicate that I should be quiet. All of a sudden a crooked smile spread over Nigel's face that seemed out of character. He turned attention towards me and said, "You've got to pay close attention today Junior. For I am moving quickly. You've been trusted with power. You've been trained well. Use what's in your hand, Moses. Leave pharaoh and his army under the weight of the sea." Whelp! That was my answer. That was my instruction. And that's my Father! I know that for sure because he called me by my nickname and these fellas didn't know it. Which further proved what God told me earlier on this porch. I'm right where I need to be, among family.

Chapter

15

<u>Dahlia</u>

Now truth be told, that was the best sleep I've had in months! I don't know what type of mattress Liberty has but you can bet your sciatic nerve I'm going to get me one. I felt like I've slept for days and I've only slept for 6 hours. My bladder woke me up with an urgency that couldn't be ignored. I get up and run to the bathroom. Running because I noticed that there was only a bra and panties covering this sexiness. I didn't want Lib's new man to see things he could never touch. I am respectful! Well most days anyway.

After my bladder finally finished raising the Pearl River, I got a good look at my frame in this floor to ceiling looking glass. I didn't like what I saw. My features are beginning to sink in in the wrong places. My face looks so "po" that my forehead seems to be protruding out. That's not me. I have been on the run for so long that I haven't stopped to notice...me. I've taken care of others for so long that I have severely neglected myself. I don't know how to stop. I'm addicted. Is that a character flaw that will cost me relationships? I want to do better. No, I'm gone have to do better. My own health depends on it. I'm going to have to start cutting folks loose and prioritize. Too much is getting too much of me. I think I'm just spread too thin. And I'm going to fix it, today. I'm going to put in for a vacation and actually take a vacation. A vacation, alone? Hmm. That's a concept that I am going to get used to. I'm never alone. I wouldn't know how to act. But that would be some great sleep. Maybe I'd have a few days to myself and then invite someone to join in the fun. "Yeah, that sounds good." The sound of my voice didn't match the person in the mirror. I honestly looked like a walking dead red light special. "Dahlia?" I heard my name in a voice that didn't belong to Liberty or anyone else I knew. "Yo" I go to get my basketball playing clothes. Easy to slip into. Liberty walks around the corner with a look on her face that says she wants to know I'm talking to.

"Libby you've got company?" She looked at me with a motherly tone of vision. "Dahlia ain't nobody here but me and you." I look her in the face for her to tell me she's just playing. I know what I heard. "Libby, no one else is here? It's just me and you. Then who just called my name?" I looked at her with a face dripped in sarcastic disbelief. "Dee, get up and look around and see for yourself. I have no reason to lie to you. Now, we will have company later on today. All the crew is coming here and I'm cooking. So we'll have a family gathering here this afternoon around 3. But as far as right now? It's just you, me, the Father, Son and Holy Ghost. You may want to go back to sleep. You've got a few more hours. You might as well get some rest." And with that she walked out of the room and closed the door. She opened it back up and told me that she has my phone so I can get some rest. I lay back on the bed and wonder. Am I losing my damn mind? I know good and well I heard my name in a stranger's mouth. I know that I'm tired, stressed, possibly pissed off at Tracey. But delusional? Naw. Can't be! Before I could further debate this issue I fell off to sleep. I'm telling you I'm getting me one of these mattresses!

Liberty's heavy hands shook me awake. I was so upset! I was in another world at complete peace. I ain't never felt that type of peace. It was almost forceful. I know that's weird but it's honest. It was all consuming. I wondered if I was dying. If that's what dying is like, why do medical professionals fight so hard to keep people alive? "Get up, sunshine. I cooked and everybody is here waiting for you to eat." Oh man, I totally forgot the company she mentioned earlier. I ran in the bathroom to make sure I looked presentable at Lib's massive table spread. Ol girl can burn when she puts her mind to it. As small as I look, I need to partake of every single thing she cooked with plans for seconds. When I walked into the dining room I was knocked off my feet. All my brothers and best friends were present and accounted for. Plus there were two fellows here that I didn't know. I was surprised and half scared. What if all these people are here to tell me something bad. What if mama's dead? I'm tripping. Libby wouldn't have cooked a whole spread. We'd have all been at the hospital. This brain of mine has got to calm down. I've got to get it together. I'm not a worrier. I'm not going to start now. Something's got to give. I'm not sure what's going on, but there is entirely too much love in this room for it to be a bad thing. Whatever it is, we'll get through it together; as a family. I'm sure of it.

"It's about time you woke up homie! This spaghetti can't wait forever." My oldest brother David said. I just looked at him with one eyebrow raised. "You bet not eat before I get up dude. You know that ain't how we roll round chea." Everybody laughed. We say grace as a family when we're together. No matter if it is me and my brothers or me and my sisters. That same rule applies. It's almost a "Fast and Furious" type tradition. I'm grateful for my family, blood and chosen. I give thanks every time we gather together. Because you never know when it will be the last time. Libby caught my eye and smiled at me with a knowing smile. It's like she read my mind and it was as if she had something up her sleeve. I'll have to ask her about that later.

Byrd caught my attention. "Dee, this is Nigel Hampton. He's the new boo." I looked him up and down in an incognito manner as I made my way over to where they were. I scoped homeboy all the way out. He's extremely handsome. Those dreads and those eyes are absolutely spellbinding. I can see why Byrd is into him.

But he's a little older than she is. She didn't sit by him in calculus, that's for sure. But he seemed to have a good vibe. She was at ease and happy. That was enough to get my approval right there. If you know Byrd, she's hard to impress. Very skeptical of everyone she meets that wants to get to know her better. "Nigel, I'm Dahlia. You good?" He blushed a little but kept a cool demeanor. "I'm good Dahlia, how are you?" His voice was just as manly and assertive as his appearance. Okay bruh bruh! "I'm good and hungry. If you are here, at this gathering we'll have plenty of time to talk and become family. I can promise you that." He looked at me with satisfaction in his eyes.

There was a knowing in his smile that made me trust him automatically. His handshake put me at ease. This brother was for my sister. He'd die for her. I could tell. Since my job caused me to be around strangers all the time you learn to read intentions, emotions and responses. This man had it bad for my baby sister and it gave me such a warm and fuzzy feeling. Looks like Libby and Byrd got themselves a forever friend. And I'm loving it.

"Can someone say grace so I can quiet the pain in my belly?" Daylan asked and Damian cosigned. I looked at Lib. It's her house so she gets to assign that responsibility. She looked at me, then at her new fellow. "Uh...is it okay if

David says grace?" All of my mama's children hollered "NO!" all at once. Byrd, Lib and Chevy laughed so hard they doubled over. He looked around at us, his betrayers with a look of shock on his face. The brother above me, Dorian Micah, spoke for the first time since I've come out of the room. "Now David? I love you and all. But you are so long winded. And um...we? We hungry. You pray later, mmkay?" We all cracked up. David even chuckled after that one. Dorian is the quietest guy I've ever known. He hardly ever just speaks his mind. And for him to say anything, especially in front of people he doesn't know, he really meant it.

Damian stepped up and said, "I'll say grace." We all bowed our heads with no argument. Partially because we know this will be sweet and short. I snuck a peak at him before he started praying. He winked at me. He makes me feel special, always has. He gives me hope by the way he looks at me. And today is no different. "Father, thank you. Thank you for this food and everybody who is standing around it. Let everyone who is present here feel like family. And Lord, let this family always be. I know a few of us feel that there are some people missing from this circle. But Lord, you know why it is only us gathered here. And we want to thank you for everything you're doing in our lives and through this food which smells so good. In Jesus' name. Amen."

My mind is reeling from his short yet effective prayer. And although I said Amen with everybody else, I can't help feeling like that prayer was for me. Tracey isn't here. I was thinking that she should be. Even though I'm slightly pissed off at her right now, I was hoping that she would fit into a gathering like this. Just about everybody in this dining room holds a piece of my heart. If Tracey holds a piece of it too, shouldn't she fit in? I love that girl. I swear I do. But these last few days seem to have been a warning of some sort. I just keep thinking about all the times I've ignored warning signs about certain people who have done such damage to my life, changed my character, or have made me cry.

Time and time again I begged God to send me a sign of warning against that type of evil. But I'll admit, I can't count how many times I've ignored those very signs I asked for when it came to Tracey. I don't want to be a hypocrite. But when it comes to her, I am. I can't tell you how many times I've told my family, "Don't let the new boo change you." Now look at me. I barely recognize myself in the mirror. I'm literally wasting away from taking care of her. This isn't love, this is neglect. But at the same time I am the one to blame for my current state, not her.

"Dahlia Daecion Emerley! Come back to planet Earth! What's on your mind so heavy Doll?" David was snapping his fingers in front of my face. I had no idea my thoughts were so loud that they'd blocked out everybody else. I really got to get a hold on things. Been off my game all day. "Sorry Dave. What were you saying?" He looked at me like he could've slapped the back of my head. That's the look that mama used to give me when I wasn't listening. Why am I missing her? I've thought about her most of the day. "I said why you so thin? I also asked what was on your mind."

I know I can trust the people at this table with these thoughts and feelings. But now just doesn't seem like it's the right time. "I've been working doubles and not eating like I should. And honestly, I've got so much on my mind I wouldn't know where to start talking." He smiled at me and patted my hand under the table. It was a fatherly knowing in that display of affection which is something I so missed. I don't get to be the kid anymore since I'm the medical leader in the bunch. I'm expected to be mature and strong at all times. David must have sensed my weariness of playing that role. It's time for me to get out of the hot seat. "Libby, gone and tell us about this new change in your life. It's more than just this sharp dressed cop you've got sitting next to you." She blushed.

Chapter

16

<u>Liberty</u>

"Gone and spill the beans." That was not what I wanted to do but I had everyone's attention thanks to Dahlia. My relationship with Adonis and with God was just now blossoming into something. I didn't want to call it out before it was time. I didn't want to jinx it. I was chewing my garlic bread in hopes to give my brain time to come up with the right things to say. I really wanted to say, "None of ya damn business!" but I'm turning over a new leaf; or so I hope. But before I could open my mouth, captain save 'em spoke up.

"Well we met a few days ago in a rather awkward way. But we spent some time together and hit it off. The rest is yet to come." Junior did that! I was proud. He answered the question but didn't give out too much information. Because no one knows about the fight/shootout that occurred at this house a few days ago and I really don't want anyone else to know. Byrd tooted out her lips in disbelief of Junior's reply. I was so hoping no one else saw that look on her face, but Adonis did. "You don't believe me Korede'?" Byrd sipped her fruit punch and cleared her throat.

She said it simply but it sounded so dramatic, "Uh...no." Adonis laughed and so did everybody else, except for me. Today was supposed to be about getting Dahlia right, not me. Byrd cleared her throat again and said, "No offense to you Mr. Officer but Lib has a way about her that commands way more attention than you just mentioned. She's much more complicated than that. So I'm hoping that one of you spills the authentic Arabica and not that instant decaf of an explanation you offered."

For the first time since she stepped in the door Chevy opened her mouth for more than the spaghetti. "Look here, I haven't had a home cooked meal in months. Liberty was gracious enough to provide this scrumptious meal of which I plan on portioning off and taking some home for lunch tomorrow. Now with that being said; Byrd shut the hell up and stop rocking this boat. Now if Mr. Officer wants to tell us that half-truth wrapped up in a bow, let him. He is trying to court. Allow the man to get on the girl's good side. Cause I don't hear you offering up any explanations about Brother Good Looking that's sitting beside you with ya messy ass. Speaking of which; Brother Good Looking? Be a gentleman and pass me them green beans, will ya?"

Chevy was on my side? I'm shocked. But the way she was talking brought me such joy. That's the Chevy I knew before the alcohol and the death of her husband. Honestly I'd say it's the Chevy I knew before High School Graduation. She was back and as funny as ever. Everybody was cracking up. The brothers were looking at both of the strange guests in a way that stated, "You're cool now but I'll kill you if I have to". Time went on as small talk became a big fuss when someone brought up basketball. I had no idea what was going on so there was no need for me to add my two cents into the conversation. I noticed that I was in good company with Byrd and Chevy. Of course Dahlia was talking noise with the best of them.

When I noticed that we women were being ignored, I motioned for them to join me in the kitchen. They grabbed plates and obliged my request. Once in the kitchen I fixed a few to go boxes. But for the most part, we threw everything out. Ain't a chance in hell I was gonna wash all of those dishes. I'm grateful for the Dollar Tree. Everything was in foil, plastic, Styrofoam, or paper. It all went in the garbage. After the kitchen was clean I told them to follow me to the back porch. They washed their hands and did as they were told. I picked the back porch because it was such a beautiful and warm spring-like day. But the reason above all our voices wouldn't be heard back in the dining room.

Sitting in the rockers out back Chevy spoke up first. "Liberty, that was some fine eating. Thank you ma'am. And sugar you put your foot in them green beans sho nuff!" We all started giggling. When Chevy starts talking like somebody's grandma we know she's serious. There was a clarity and a peace to Ms. Shevelle Marie that I haven't seen in such a long time. It was a welcomed difference. And I'm not the only person who noticed either. Byrd had tears in her eyes when she grabbed Chevy and hugged her. "I missed this side of you Chevrolet. Don't ever let her go away again, okay?" I started giggling again because Byrd is the only person alive who calls her that. She pulled away from Byrd and smacked her on the shoulder with a big smile on her face.

She grabbed both of our hands and said, "Y'all I'm sorry. I've allowed the troubles of life to dictate my actions, affections, my way of living. I won't do that again. But thank y'all so much for hanging in there with me. I'm not going to say that things will get better from here on out. But I will be present from now on." She hugged me and kissed Byrd on the head. "Now, can somebody tell me what we are really here for? Something is up with the two of you and your new men. Dahlia can't seem to keep her shit together. She's all over the place. Seems like it's hard for her to focus on simple things, like the conversations going on around her. And Liberty you called this meeting, which is something you don't usually do. Plus all of Marjorie Santana Emerley's sons are sitting around your table looking like the cast on Power; handsome and dangerous. So will y'all quit keeping me in suspense? Spit it out!"

I closed my eyes and took a deep breath. I opened my mouth to speak and closed it when I felt a hand on my arm. Byrd had a look in her eyes and an expression on her face that she knew way more than I did. She started with the story. "Long story short y'all, Tracey isn't who she said she was. And she has harmful intentions toward Dee. She's been gearing up for this ambush for years. I don't know all of the details, but I know enough. Nigel was a sorcerer who was paid to do things...favors, if you will, for other people. That's how he made his living. Well Na'Treiel was a client of his for years. She's married to his older brother." Chevy and I both said "Married?" at the same time.

We were both knocked back. That was way more information than what I had. I knew the girl was foolin' with witchcraft, but Byrd had all the goods. She went on. "Yeah y'all, married. And has been for quite some time. I'm talking years! Well apparently she's had a root put on her husband so that he would believe everything she says. He works offshore, in Africa. And he's gone for months at a time. That's when she does her, when he's at work. So come to find out that she's your sister." She pointed at me. I broke the circle. I had to. I went in the house to get a drink. Because of that statement I knew this was the day for all the secrets to come out. I wasn't sure I was ready for it. But if I put my trust in the Lord and a shot of courage in my system, there's nothing that I couldn't do. I went to the cabinet for the Belvedere, mixed it with the fruit punch Chevy had made, and headed back out to the pack porch. When I returned both ladies were looking at me wide eyed.

"I needed a drink for the stories to be told. I'm sorry Chevy. I know you're trying to do better and normally I wouldn't do something like this in front of you. Just think of it as medicine. Because I'm going to need this to get through the day." Chevy nodded her head in understanding. "Lib, I'm the one with the problem, not you. So if this is what you need at your house, then this is what you do. I'm alright. I'd tell you if I wasn't. Now I need for you to explain to me how this heifer is your sister? Because that statement only seemed to shock me. Which means you knew all along, didn't you?"

I took a long hard swig of the pretty concoction in my left hand, which was very good might I add. "I didn't know that Tracey was my sister. I'm not surprised though. My sperm donor had many children. I don't know them all. I don't want to know any of them. Go ahead Byrd, finish what you know." Now Byrd is the cool headed one. But she was clearly getting upset. She didn't even know the story but her sensitive nature is starting to feel my sense of dread about revealing these secrets. "Well, for some reason she thinks that Dahlia has something to do with the death of her dad; well y'alls dad. She's come to hurt Dee in attempts to avenge the man's death." Chevy spoke up next.

"So this dumb ass broad has been wasting her time trying to find out what happened to her father and decided to pick out Dahlia, of all people, to blame. Hasn't she figured out that Dee tries to help people? She wouldn't kill nobody. Fight em, maybe. But not kill. Why in the hot hell did this girl..." I had to cut her off. I raised my hand in a stop traffic manner and went ahead and allowed my liquid courage to do its thing. "Chevy, it's true." They both looked at me with mouths wide open. Tears started to trickle down Byrd's face. I didn't want to tell them; I felt like it wasn't mine to tell. But I guess it has to be done if we're going to help Dahlia out of this mess that Terry Dawkins' sorry ass put her in.

"The day we put my mama in the ground Terry, the sperm donor, raped me. Dahlia caught him in the beginning of it and she put a bullet in his head while he was on top of me. We were both around 13 so it was a juvenile court matter. Those records were sealed. We never really spoke about it again. There wasn't a reason to. When the cops showed up and saw what they saw, it confirmed our story. They had to pull the man off of me. It was open and shut. That's why Dee and I are so close. She saved me. That's why you two can fight. Because we had to fight to survive. We wanted you to be able to do the same. We are all well trained in several forms of combat. The only area where we're inexperienced is spiritual warfare. That's what Tracey is good at. She blindsided us. We have to knock her flat on her ass because she is messing with family."

By now Chevy has joined Byrd in crying. I'm not crying. I'm tired of crying. However I am shaking. An old secret has been brought to the light. I've been freed by telling my "sisters" my story. Had I known it would've been this liberating I would've told it to them years ago. I feel like I just had a breath of fresh air for the first time in years.

"So what do we need to do?" That was a simple question with a complicated answer asked by an emotionally charged Chevy. I simply shrugged my shoulders. David came out on the porch with Byrd's new boo. In that moment David said something that forever changed my perspective on men, "You let the men handle it. You ladies aren't ready for this type of carrying on but we men are."

Chapter

17

<u>David</u>

In all my years of living, never did I believe I'd be here joining forces with my brothers, blood and blood bought, to fight for the soul of my sister. And to battle her lover no less. But here I am, ready and willing to do whatever it takes. Love causes you to do more than you're willing to. Love will make a peaceful man go to war. It's not like I don't know that she brought this trouble to herself by loving on someone with her eyes shut. Dahlia was stupid for this. Plain and simple. But I can't say that I haven't been stupid like this at least once or twice a year for a few years. I expected this behavior from my brothers. It's unfair that I put different expectations on my sister. But I did.

I feel I've done all I need to do to prepare for such a time as this. But it doesn't stop my mind from wandering if I left something out. I know those that I stand with have the same mindset as I do. I was worried about Nigel at first. I didn't know him from Adam. But as I watched him I was reminded of a night of revival service I attended in New Orleans a year ago. The pastor had an altar call and Nigel went up there. He had tears on his face and a wild look in his eyes. Brother looked like he was at his wits end. The pastor prayed for him and said that his days ahead will be sho'nuff rough because Satan wanted him to stay on the path he was on. The preacher said, the devil was going to try and kill' em simply cause he didn't wanna lose 'em. But if he really wanted to change for the better, he'd fight for his life. Said that if he lived through the next 2 months of hell, he could make it through anything. I remember closing my eyes and praying for this dude's strength. I kept hoping he'd be alright. I remember God saying to me that night, "Don't worry about him, you'll see him emerge scarred but strong."

Here I am at my sister's best friend's house sitting at the dinner table right next to who God called strong. I feel privileged. I know what he used to do. Instead of judging him for it, I'm glad he can lend his experiences and the wisdom of his old ways of livelihood. When you have someone you love in such a shape as this, you'll accept help however you can get it. I'm glad he was willing. He's the one that got her in this predicament and hopefully he knows how to get her out. For those of you out there who don't know about magick, there's always a loophole...a way of escape if you will. You never cast something that has no exception clause. If your shadow man tells you any different, he lying for the profit and you bet not trust em no more.

This fella that's with Libby has so much power sitting in his chest and his hip that we could all go home; he could win this battle all on his own. He's got the compassion of Christ in his eyes and the stir of the Holy Ghost in his touch. He shook my hand when he arrived at Libby's house, and it took all the man I am not to cry, confess my sins, and beg for forgiveness. That bulge in his back and in his ankle wasn't lost on me either. I respect a man with authority in his character and in his holster. He's got to be headed for the pulpit soon. That type of fire doesn't make sense to just waste it on a cop with no calling. Nigel and I informed Adonis of what was going down. The smile that came across his face was puzzling at first. But then he said "The Lord introduced me to the love of my life a few days ago." Pointing to Libby. "And she turns around and introduces me to my brothers." Pointing to us. "Y'all might think I'm crazy, but this is a divine set up. You can count on me. Whatever you need, I'm your boy. Swear." I promise you those words and the power in his eyes reassured me that this plan was not going to backfire.

For the task that lies ahead, I decided to study everybody. I needed to make sure I knew my surroundings well. I need no surprises. I noticed that Libby and Chevy have changed significantly and for the better. Chevy wasn't drunk and Libby wasn't high on...Libby. Since her old man's demise, Chevy has been a train wreck. Her aura's been all over the place and so has her emotions. Always been one to speak her mind, but lately there's been no tact in her demeanor. However, today she looks like she's back in control. She doesn't smell like she wasted a bottle of perfume on her clothes. She looks in charge, level headed, and well…saved. It's a good look. Libby looks like she just met Jesus in the lonesome valley, and he was taking names. There's a look she has in her eyes that I've never seen before, and I've known Libby almost all of her life. She looks like she's made peace with her past and plans for her future. It's a beautiful thing and it looks like Adonis is the reason. If he can perform that miracle in Libby in a few days I can only imagine what he can do with a church in a few years. I hope Libby can hold on to this joy she's found when she finds out she'll be a pastor's wife. Who am I kidding? Libby? In fancy suits, high heels, designer purses, hair always done and consistently in the limelight; that's right up her alley.

Byrd has evolved into a very beautiful bulldog. The aggression that has consumed her these past few months has to be because of her job and school. She has always been smart, observant and ready to defend herself if need be. But as of late, she seems to want to take the fight to you instead of waiting for it. That type of behavior can get her into a whole lot of trouble if she can't handle it. And of course by handling it, I mean not allowing it to handle you. I do hope that Nigel can help her put a reign on that attitude. Teach her to use it as fuel and not fire. I'm sure he will. He looks at her like his heart is singing "ain't nothing out there for me, she the only one that I love". He's a little older than I would've picked for her. But honestly she needs that stability and wisdom. After she lost her folks she lost her sense of direction. In all honesty that is expected. But she never took the time to care for herself after the funeral. She went into survival mode and did what needed to be done not realizing that there was a deep emotional wound that needed tending to. Regardless of what most people say, time doesn't heal all things. You've got to be the one in control of the healing most of the time.

I looked at my brothers. They are just as goofy as they always are when they get around one another. We're a tight knit group of siblings. But there is one thing I did notice about Baybro. He's missing his mama. Damian Marsal is the last of the clan. He's the one that experienced the most changes with Marjorie. I don't call her mama because she isn't one. Marjorie needed more attention and taking care of when Damian was home. She's sick. I'll admit, some of that is my fault. I may or may not have prayed a certain prayer or two that led to her suffering. I'm trying to get Marjorie out of hell. If she's too sick to act up, maybe she'll repent and start acting right. When Baybro moved out and left her sickly behind alone for good, I just knew that this was the beginning of a turnaround.

I was wrong. She called me, told me that I better come home and take care of her or else. That was the first time I cussed Marjorie smooth out.

My voice was low, my enunciation was on point and I was very glad I wasn't in her presence at that moment. I could've hit her. I don't condone violence from a man to a woman. But I would've gladly done a nickel to a dime for beating her within inches of her foul life. Since then, we don't speak of or to each other. I honestly think that all of our relationships with Marjorie convinced Baybro to cut ties with her. He knew it would only be a matter of time before his story started to sound like ours. He knew we all had his back. But I think he cut ties too soon. His heart is a little heavy with need for a mama. I just hate that he'll have to get that need met by his wife. Only Dorian has found his wife. He's proposed, but no wedding date as of yet. We all treat her like she's a queen. She's one of the sweetest people you'll ever meet. She's also one dedicated soldier. She's missing this family dinner now because she's gone to drill this weekend. Whoever the poor ladies are that marries the rest of us, will have to be able to put up with quite a lot of damaged goods.

Now that I think about it, Doll has shut her eyes to the tricks of Tracie because she just wants the love of a mama. It's all starting to make sense now. Of all the relationships she's had, none of them were as serious as this one because she's starting to make peace with who she is; a motherless child. She needs someone to fill the void Marjorie left inside of her heart. Most of the women that Doll found interest in, was a way of getting back at Marjorie. A state of rebellion if you will. But most of the women and the men for that matter just used her. They didn't try to take care of her the way Tracie did. Tracie was trying to get a way in to hurt her so she played on Doll's emotional weaknesses. That heifer! I'm beginning to understand how she was able to get in the door now. The more you understand a problem, the more equipped you are to solve it.

Aunt Jessie told me, "If you can call that thing by its name you can shame it and kill it at the root. If you don't know its name you can't uproot it. If you don't uproot it, you won't kill it." I plan on killing it at the root at all costs. Don't get me wrong, I don't want to harm this girl. But I'm not above killing her. I've killed men and women whose names I didn't know; who has done nothing to me. But they had to die for the sake of my country and it was my duty to make it happen. I've got no issues killing a woman who had every intention of killing my sister. But my sister and I will have a heart to heart once this ordeal is over. She needs to make some difficult choices about what she's willing to deal with and who she's willing to lose. I've never seen her so small. She's not eating. Dark circles under her eyes let me know she's not resting. Her skin isn't as smooth and her toes are not painted. That indicates personal neglect. She's throwing herself aside to care for others. That I'm used to, just not to this extent. Dahlia Daecion has been choosing everybody else over herself just like Marjorie has done to her all of her life. She thinks that quality makes her a caring, loving person. If taken out of context it makes you a fool and a doormat. Love and abuse looks the same depending on the view from where you're standing.

As we boys are sitting around the table talking sports with Dahlia, I notice that the ladies of the group have exited stage left. They used to do that all the time when we'd get to the subject of "ball" at the family gathering. But today there is something different. Maybe it's because of the purpose of the gathering. Maybe it's because they've changed. Whatever the reason, I need to go and spy on their conversation. But I have to play it smooth. I can't just jump up and go. I'll cause alarm to the rest of the crowd, especially Doll. While I'm sitting concocting a plan, Nigel nodded at me and tilted his head in the direction of the kitchen. I couldn't do anything but smile. God worked that out real quick. I stood and walked into the kitchen, Nigel followed close behind.

"Uh...where did the ladies go?" He had every intention of protecting not only Byrd, but all the women in the house. I liked that. He's gaining my respect more and more by the minute. "They usually leave the men to talk about sports at these events. But something seems weird to me and I can't shake that feeling." He nodded with a look of 'I feel you' etched into his face. Then he said, "I felt a draft when they left. The winds of revelation are blowing. They're out there telling each other the truth." He nodded towards the kitchen window. I could see the top of the rocking chairs moving. My heart became so full of love for Chevy that it began to make my chest heavy. Not a romantic love, but a sisterly love. Don't get me wrong, all the women in this house are drop dead gorgeous and I'd be lucky to have either of them on my arm. But this heavy pain in my chest; this is what the love of the Father feels like when someone chooses him. I mindlessly grabbed my chest. Nigel took one look at my face and chuckled with a voice of experience..."Well don't let me stop you David. Go on and show her what the love can do."

Chapter

18

<u>Chevy</u>

God! It's only 4:30 pm. I've had the most wind knocked out of me in a thirty minute period than I have in years! I haven't had a drink in days but God knows I need one. Liberty was raped! By her father no less. What is it with these sick sons of bitches! Why is it that our black men are raping or taking advantage young girls? In the history of black women as slaves, don't they know that their ancestral grandmother was raped? How does that make you any better than the white master? That makes me mad! You let the devil talk you into something so foul. But if that same thing had happened to your sister, your daughter, your mother; you'd be ready to kill. That's the stupidest, dumbest, shitty-est behavior and mindset known to man. And Dahlia killed him! She shot his hellish ass right in the head, AT 13!

I remember all the cops racing past the church to get to Lib's aunt's house. I thought it was a car wreck. I didn't think anything of it. I was there at the funeral. My mom knew Lib's mom. I was 10 or 11 at the time. Oh and there's a blood thirsty whore out there wanting to kill my Dahlia over her ignorant father's death! Oh I'm down for whatever. I'm ready for this fight. I need to know what to do and when to do it. One thing I can do is sharp shooting. I'll lay on my belly on a rooftop for this here! I'm so mad I feel like I've drunk gasoline. I'm hot all over! Even though I'm spontaneous combustible hot I feel sorry for Lib. First time ever by the way. In the past few years, all I've known is selfish and snobby. I've felt as if she felt like she was entitled to accomplishments that she never worked for. Now I know that was just a cover up to hide the worthlessness she felt due to her rough upbringing. She's had it hard. We've all been there for her for years. But I didn't know we were the only ones.

I figured her whole family was an actual family. That just goes to show that you should never judge a book by its cover. And just because you know doesn't mean you know everything. We've been rocking and rolling for I know 20 years and I never knew any of this. We need a girl's week to just tell it all. Get it all out of our system. Give ourselves the chance to be there for one another. Instead of insisting that we go through life and its hardships all alone.

But these menfolk around here done stepped up to the plate. Saying "Let the men handle it" like we're actually going to let them do all the heavy lifting. Oh but no! I want my turn at bat. Every person in this house has some type of combat or weapons training. I think it's only fair that we all get to have a lick. But there's one thing that Liberty said that has me worried. "The only area where we're inexperienced is spiritual warfare." Never have I ever heard a truer statement. Just as I began to panic David came and knelt in front of my rocking chair and hugged me. He whispered in my ear a scripture I've heard before but never understood, "For the weapons of our warfare are not carnal, but mighty through God to the pulling down of strong holds".

For the first time in my life I felt the need to give God control of the situation. I mean, I've prayed and asked God to fix it; the mess I've made. But to really be willing to completely step out of the way and put my thoughts and feelings aside to give God the reigns of control? Never been my cup of tea. But the feeling to do so was so overwhelming because I have absolutely no idea what to do to fix it. I could just kill the girl but it'll only kill her. And yet her death might not be enough to stop her plans of destroying Dahlia. I can't have that. I can deal with a lot of things except not knowing if and or when harm is coming to someone I love. I can handle being hurt by my own actions. That is a part of living. What goes up must come down. You will reap what you sow. However this thing here with Tracy is more than my brain can fathom. It's not normal. Her wanting Dahlia to pay for her father's sins is a bit much.

David started talking and somehow my soul responded without the use of my mouth or my mind. Tears begin to trickle down my face. He said, "Chevy, God is bigger than anything you've ever seen. He's better than anything you've ever had. You've flirted with the idea of God without actually getting to know Him. He is nothing like the church portrays him to be. He's bigger than any box they can put Him in. You've been changing for the better lately. And that's good! I'm so proud of you. But how about you change permanently? Let this great big God be more than a Sunday's tradition. Accept Him for who He is. Let Him live in you." I just held on to him as he talked to a part of me that was willing to listen. Usually, I'm the one who is off the porch and into the car by the time someone starts talking "Jesus".

But apparently by these tears riding down my cheeks I needed it. I wanted it. I felt something inside me open up. I felt no fear; no pain. No hesitations. I felt relief all over me. I wanted this God he was talking about. I have been in church all of my life and I never met Him. I wanted what David had. It seemed like David knew him personally. As if they were friends. Like they talk on the regular. All I could do was nod my head yes. I didn't trust my mouth. I knew that if my lips parted ways then the ugly cry would have permission to come forth like Lazarus from the grave. That cry is reserved for the privacy of my own home.

David put his hands on my face. His thumbs dried my tears. He prayed for me or should I say with me. I was praying inside my heart. I felt like God heard me. I felt different after the prayer than before it. I still wanted to kill Tracy but not as much. I didn't expect to have forgiveness in my heart for Tracy that quickly. I'm not rushing God. That song said you can't hurry God, you just have to wait. On that I can wait, I promise you.

When I got enough nerve to look David in the face he was smiling at me; a "big brother punched the neighborhood bully over his sister" type of smile. It was mischievous. It made me feel loved, valued, worth fighting for. If this is what real Christian living is all about, I'm in. Maybe not all in at this present moment. There is a chick that needs killing...I mean stopping. Cut me some slack. "Baby steps Chev. One thing at a time. You hang with me, and you'll be just fine." Oh but no! Is he hearing my thoughts now? Dave...you doing the most, ain't cha? He fell out laughing at me. "Close your mouth Chevy. You gone let the flies in."

How is it that in that time frame the whole world stood still? There wasn't a car rolling down the street. There wasn't a side conversation on the porch. Everyone who was on the porch before this literal 'come to Jesus' meeting was there when it was over. But somehow it was just David, God, and I. I've never had an experience that completely captured all of my attention to the point where even time seemed to have slowed to a halt.

"Excuse me Colonel, just exactly how are you men prepared for this?" Byrd interrupted my thoughts with a very good question. David looked at Byrd with a smirk, then at me with such certainty and said; "We Emerley boys have a great aunt that we spent summers with down in New Orleans, then over in Shreveport when a storm blew her house away. Dahlia wasn't allowed to go because that wasn't her aunt, it was ours. Jessica Diane Malone taught us more than just spells and potions. She taught us how to depend on the God they shout about on Sunday mornings. 'There's a delicate balance' she used to tell us. When we all turned 14 we were introduced to m-a-g-i-c-k, white and gray. We were taught certain practices and histories. We were told that this was our heritage and that we should be proud but not boastful. Even though we didn't deal with black magick as children, I did dabble in it as an adult. I'm not good at it and it didn't make me feel good about myself. So I stuck to what I was taught. Now as far as white and gray, or hoodoo as it's popularly known, I'm very good at it. And with the help of Nigel and Adonis, we're going to take good care of Dahlia. I don't want to kill this girl, but if it comes down to her or my sister..." He took a deep breath and let it out slow..."She'll just have to go.

Baby...a cold child ran throughout my being; it made me shiver and made my teeth chatter. Nigel looked at me and smiled. And in his thick accent he said, "Don't be alarmed. I asked God to show me a sign that Tracy was coming here looking for Dahlia. That was my sign. Winds of change are headed this way." All I could do was nod my head in the direction the wind was coming from. I was shivering and yawning so hard that tears were rolling down my face. David got off the floor of the porch and started rubbing my shoulders trying to warm me up. David nodded to Nigel.

Nigel said with a New Orleans accent and a protective authority that made me feel like Byrd would always be safe. "Ladies, it's time to move inside. The show's getting ready to start."

Chapter

19

<u>Byrd</u>

We all moved inside from the back porch. I was so nervous! I knew that something big was going to happen. I also knew that I wasn't going to be of much help during this big event. I was a basket of butterflies. My nerves were everywhere. Nigel was standing by the door when he noticed that I couldn't keep my hands still. He lovingly grabbed my hands and took me back outside. He told David to give him a minute. He looked in my eyes and said "I've got you. Your presence is enough. You don't have to do anything, but be here." I nodded my head, but it didn't stop the feeling of pure trouble inside of my being.

"Korede'?" I said, "Yeah?" He grabbed me and said "Clear". Then he kissed me. Y'all I've got to get used to this kissing! My knees started to wobble. He backed up from me and said "Byrd, concentrate." He kissed me again. I concentrated on his lips, his touch, and the way he smelled. Then he broke the kiss again and led me back into the house. I noticed that when I stepped back in the doorway all the nervousness was gone. I was a lot more confident. I had no apprehensions about what was about to go down. He took it away. I looked back at him. He winked at me. I smiled and started telling God, thank ya. He set me up with someone who could love me enough to take away the nervousness, the fear, the anxiety of living. Someone who would push me to enjoy being me. Someone I could love and lean on to help and not hinder for selfish gain. I was so happy that God loved me enough to provide in such a way. I wanted to laugh out loud. I was so happy. I finally got what Nigel was trying to tell me on the night we met.

"You'll get what you want but it won't be enough to keep you satisfied." If I did what I thought was best for me I wouldn't have given Nigel a chance because school and money came first. He would have been a distraction. But, if I didn't I wouldn't have ever known that Dahlia was in danger. I would've never forgiven myself if something had happened to Dahlia and I could've prevented it in some way. My life would forever be changed and I would've had a falling out with God because he already took my parents away. But he gave me a family to look after me and hold me up when I needed it. If he took her away too...I just don't know.

God led me here because he wanted me here. He'll tell me what to do when He's ready for me to do something. I have to keep reminding myself that all this is His business and not mine. I'm just glad I was thought of to be used to help Dahlia. And I'll help in any way that I can. David got everyone's attention. "Yo! Everybody, we need to talk some serious talk." The Emerley children immediately stopped talking and looked at the elder amongst their clan. David in turn looks directly at Dahlia. "Doll, you're in some danger and that's why we are all here." She looked at him with pure shock. She pointed to herself and mouthed 'me'. David nodded his head up and down rather slowly.

I guess Dee had to process what David was saying. He carried on. "Your lovely spouse has some secrets. Those secrets being her intention and her identity. But you were so happy being boo'd up that you didn't realize there was some stuff about her that you didn't know." She was getting upset. I could tell by the vein in her neck. All I'm saying is that if the men are going to handle it, they need to handle it with care. He continued. "Tracy is married...to Nigel's brother." Dahlia's mouth dropped open and she looked right at Nigel in the most apologetic manner possible. Then she shook her head in hopes that the news she just received wasn't actually true. She was hurt. One thing that we girls stand by is our standards. One of our standards is no married partners. That's why we started ragging on Liberty so hard when she started seeing married men. And she knew we'd kill for her, but it was the principle of the matter. That's why she kept it secret until she couldn't and needed our help. Dahlia covered her face in shame.

"Doll, there is so much more." I could hear her moan. "Tracy, your love, put an obsession root on you." Her head jerked up and looked him in his face. She was mad as fire. "A what?!" She exclaimed. "Naw, naw, naw! You got that wrong David. Can't be. She wouldn't do me this way. Why would she do me this to me?" Damien was sitting beside her and placed his hand on her knee in support. David answered her by saying, "I found a jar under your bed. It contained red rose petals, red silk thread, two pictures, one of you and one of her, gun powder and hair that I assumed belonged to her. Tied to the jar was a tag that read 'Dahlia's undoing'. I found it right after you called me yesterday morning. I took it outside and smashed it against a brick which caused it to catch fire. I had to break that curse off you. That jar, that tag, and the fact that she knew I was at your house even though I hadn't seen her made me very uneasy."

The words 'Dahlia's undoing' really scared me. I started to shake. Tracy was seriously trying to hurt my sister. And had gotten close enough to do it. She had a key to the house! I held on to Nigel. He needed to know that I was so glad that he's here. Dahlia began to cry. No sound, just tears. "Doll it gets worse." David said it in an empathetic tone. "She's here to avenge her father's death. She's Libby's older sister." Dahlia wailed out loud. This is an issue none of us knew about until today. We didn't know how she felt about what she had to do. We didn't know if she'd put it behind her; if she'd dealt with it or not. But by that sound that escaped her throat, she was taunted by it. Liberty rushed over to her and hugged her tight. Dahlia held on to her for dear life. Tears flooded my face. You could hear the pain and the sadness. It was like those two grown women were little girls again. Dahlia started saying, "I couldn't let him hurt you Lib. I had to help you. I had to help you Libby! But I was too late! I tried so hard to get there. I was too late. He was hurting you. I had to stop him from hurting you! I couldn't think of anything else to do. He was a man and we were just little girls. I didn't know what else to do...I had to keep you safe! Your mama was gone and it's always been me and you. Libby! Libby! I had to make him stop. You okay Lib? You alright? Lib! Liberty?!"

Chevy and I ran over to where they were to hug them like we usually do when one of us is hurting. All the men just moved out the way and watched the women wail. We all needed one another. For the longest time we were all we had. We were all crying. In that moment we were all children who were dealt a rough hand. We held on to one another tight. So tight that we were trying to hug the pain away. After a few minutes, Dahlia's breathing came back to normal.

Our breathing returned to normal as well. We were finally able to let go of one another's bodies, but we still held hands. We sat on the sofa together.

We looked at David whose face was wet with tears. "Doll?" She looked at him with sadness and weight in her eyes. "I'm so sorry you went through that by yourself. You didn't have a mama and by then your dad had died. I was gone to the military and the rest of these boys were just that, boys. You had to go through all this alone. But you did nothing wrong. You did what you had to do to keep Libby safe. Nobody in this house disagrees with that, including the resident cop." David nodded his head in Adonis' direction. "You didn't have protection then. But you've got it now. Look around you. Nothing but love. We've got you Doll, all of us." She looked around at everyone. She was gaining strength from what she saw. She needed forgiveness, acceptance, and love from every pair of eyes she came in contact with. I believe she got it. When she looked at me there was a settled peaceful strength that wasn't there before.

I think we gone be alright. I think we all need to go to therapy when this is all over. We've got some issues to deal with that are bigger than anything a girl's trip will ever fix. Dahlia spoke a truth that resonated through my soul. I could feel the buzz through my skin. "I want help. I want to change. It's obvious that I need it. I put you all in a position I don't want you in. I love all y'all. Even the new boos. Y'all have shown me a support that I don't deserve, especially from you Nigel. I'm sleeping with your brother's wife. I'm so sorry! Please know that I didn't know." He nodded and patted his chest. That made me smile. Dahlia needed that. She continued. "David I want to change. But I'm not sure how. I'm not sure I'm ready to give up women. I don't know what to do. But I know God is going to have to step in and shield me from the mess I created for myself. David smiled at her and said, "Meet the resident cop and preacher. Officer Adonis Calloway."

Liberty's boo stepped up and I promise you I felt like we'd just sang 'Amazing Grace' and the pastor was fired up and about to deliver the message on a Sunday morning. This man here had some kind of relationship with God. I want to be that confident. He started to talk and my knee started bobbing up and down. I looked to my left and Chevy's leg was doing the same thing. "Dahlia, come stand in front of me." I looked to my right and Lib was crying. I swear it looked like we were on the third pew on second Sunday after the choir just showed out. Adonis took her hands and continued. "Dahlia, Jesus loves you. You need to rest in that and love Him back. He's known who you are, what you've done, what and who you prefer and that has not changed His love for you. So why have you allowed all of that to change your love for Him? Ah...cause people talk. People got lips and they will run them. What does that have to do with you and Him? What you need to do is remember the feeling of and run towards His love. It consumes you...completely. As far as you and women go; stop worrying about it. Allow the love of God to draw you closer to Him. In your obedience to God you will develop self-control. Self-control will start to strip away your desires of everything that isn't like Him. That comes in time. Until it comes natural, you do what you know is right because it's right to do. Take life day by day. Rely on your support system. But if you want this you can have it. Dahlia, Jesus loves you. Do you want Him?"

All eyes fell on Dahlia. This was the beginning or the end of a thing. Her answer was the deciding factor in her life or her death. If the answer was no, then Tracy has won. Her experience in devilment was the weapon that took Dahlia down and was truly her undoing. I think we were all holding our breath waiting on Dahlia's answer. She was just a crying. Not a sob, just tears. "Yes, I want Him." That's all the tears would allow her broken voice to speak. Adonis said, "Okay. Well let's pray then. Everybody who can hear my voice needs to start praying. This is more than just getting Dahlia straight. We've got to wage war in the realm of the Spirit. There are few of you who know exactly what you are doing.

And there are a few who have no idea and maybe you feel like you are a hindrance. If you can pray, you belong here. If you can praise, you belong here. If you love Dahlia then your love will figure out what to do. But if you are in here you need to participate. David and Nigel I need you to guard the front door and the back door. Allow nothing to permeate or penetrate that's not supposed to be here. I know Tracy is soon to drive up, but that gives us plenty of time for us to make it comfortable enough for the King of Glory to come in." He started laughing and said with a loud boom in his voice, "Who is the King of Glory? He's the Lord strong and mighty." I started to feel like we were seriously in church. Dahlia's brothers started clapping and talking like the old deacons used to do when I was a little girl. Adonis looked at Liberty, motioned for her to join him and continued. "Who is the King of Glory? He's the Lord God mighty in battle. Free your voices and talk noise about your God." I was truly lost. Chevy was saying something about, "God I know you didn't put all this together just for this not to work." I was holding on to Chevy.

That's the only thing I knew to do. I wanted this to go smoothly. I was just lost. So I did what I do...I watched. Adonis was praying with and for Dee. Liberty was hugging Dahlia from behind with her face on her back and she was praying too. David was talking and pointing. I couldn't hear what he was saying or figure out who he was talking to. The Emerley Boys were pacing and praying with tears running down their faces. Nigel was crying and I could read his lips. He was repeating "Thank you so much Father". Chevy started saying a little something different now. She was saying "I can't wait to start my journey with you. You've done so much for me. I owe you so much. I plan on giving you as much of me as you can stand. I'm so thankful you love me, drunk and all." I started smiling. Chevy is Chevy; saved or not the girl's got a way with words. I still didn't know what to do. I closed my eyes and soaked up the atmosphere.

Chapter

20

<u>Adonis</u>

When David called me up there in the form of "The resident cop and Preacher" I honestly didn't know how to take it. But I do know that when I started talking to Dahlia it felt right. It felt too right. I never wanted to preach. I only want to help people. That's why I became a cop. I love helping people. This was no different. I felt in my element. This is my wheelhouse. When I asked her to come stand in front of me, something inside of me stood up and proclaimed the spot of control and I became a preacher. It wasn't like I accepted a calling, I think my soul stepped into an anointing that I never noticed existed. My vocal chords made my lips move. My brain was never invited into this process.

The more I talked the more I felt the presence of the God my father and grandfather spoke about. This thing was real and it had taken over me. I had no objection; none at all. As everyone was praying and praising I couldn't help but watch my surroundings. This atmosphere could breed miracles, signs and wonders. I heard the Spirit of God say, "And it will. I will use you to do one right now." Thunder boomed through my chest. My eyes fell on Byrd. She had her eyes closed. I could tell she was lost but she was so glad to be here in this atmosphere. Again my lips obeyed my voice box without my mind's consent. "Byrd, come here." She opened her eyes and came up to where I was.

I let Dahlia's hands go. She and Liberty were working this out by themselves. I grabbed hold of Byrd's hands and looked her dead in her eyes. She was nervous. My heart became so full of love for her. It was as if God formed a bloodline between the two of us at that very moment. She became my baby sister and I her big brother. "Byrd, open up and let it be." She looked at me and was hesitant but she closed her eyes and tilted her head back. She started to cry. I could feel that she'd opened up her heart for a God that she loved, but wasn't quite sure how to show it. I lifted her hands and let them go. Her body shook from the crying. I stepped closer to her so that she could hear me.

"Open your mouth Kamdyn Korede'. Let it come out. Even if it's just a sound and not a word. It'll sound mighty good to me." She opened her mouth and all I heard was "I love you too." My heart warmed immensely. It was pure. I put one hand on her stomach and the other on her back. I started praying for her to hear the Lord clearly for herself. There's no other gift like it.

After I finished praying, God led me to Chevy. I walked over to where she was sitting and sat beside her. I hugged her and said, "I love you drunk and all." She laughed through her tears and hugged me back. I told her "You'll see what you are supposed to see when it's time. But you will see. It's a little early for me to give you everything at once. You just keep talking to me. The bottle or that man you married will never hold you back again. I've covered you all your life Shevelle Marie. As long as you put me where I'm supposed to be, which is first, you have nothing to worry about." She held me tight and cried. She was free of the one thing no one wanted to discuss, the death of her husband. I worked on the case a little. It was a mess. He was a mess. I can see how he, his living and his death overshadowed her. I could hear the sound of metal hitting concrete. That was the chain that connected her to her husband being released from her soul. I heard another one hit. That was her dependence on, addiction to, and obsession with liquor.

God is showing out in the house with these women today. I let Chevy go, got up and walked back towards Nigel. He needed to go be a supportive force for his wife to be. I'll cover the door while he does his civic duty. I touched him on his shoulder. His eyes popped open. He was so lost in worship that he had to remember where he was. I told him, "I've got the door. Your wife needs a push to get in the position she's meant for. Handle ya biz homie." He smiled at me. He wiped his face and walked towards Byrd. I leaned against the door and closed my eyes. I started talking to God out loud.

"God, you have surprised me on today! You gave me a family I didn't know I needed and pushed me into a calling I didn't know I had. I was just expecting a calm dinner with just info being passed to and fro. You are amazing. Greater than anything I've ever known. Your plan isn't mine, but I trust yours before my own any day. Your knowledge supersedes any rival intelligence whether of this realm or the next. Pour out your spirit on all the flesh represented here. It is evident by the collective wail in this room you are wanted, needed, and required of the souls present. We thirst for you. We chase after you. Today we beg for the change needed to make you happy. Shake our souls. Shake our mindset. God shake our lives letting loose everything that's there that doesn't belong. We are ready and begging. We choose you the way you've chosen us. Fill us! Fill us oh God with wisdom, with power, with love. Fill us with you. It's your time to shine, allow us to be your vessels."

It was at that time that I heard Byrd speaking in tongues. I knew it was her without opening my eyes. It was sweet and pure and full of power. But what came after made me open my eyes and my mouth. Every single one of Dahlia's brothers started talking in tongues one at a time until it was a chorus. It was the exact same language. The exact same words. In all my years of living I have never witnessed that before. They were literally all on one accord. When Liberty turned around and looked at me I could see a light transfer from Byrd to her and she joined the chorus. After it lit her on fire it jumped on Nigel. Nigel then extended his hand to Chevy. When Chevy took it her whole being began to glow. She looked at me for approval like a little sister does her big brother.

I said, "Open up your mouth Chevy. Let your lips move." She closed her eyes and she joined this beautiful experience that was going on in this house. God told me to leave my post and go and get Dahlia. She and I were the only ones who weren't talking. I grabbed her hand and lead out to the middle of the room. "Dahlia, listen." She was shaking and listening. She looked at me with a question in her eyes. "God said that evil can't get through that. That sound is a hedge of protection around you. That's why they are all saying the same thing. God said you are protected to an extent that you'll never understand. In this moment hell has backed down and the sting of the fight is over. Look at what good came out of a bad situation. Look around you. This is what they all needed. And so did you. You've come back home and these children of mine have allowed me to have my way."

She looked at me and you could see the weight lift right off of her soul. She said to me in the voice of a little girl, "He can have me too. I need him to have me too, Adonis." I grabbed her in an embrace. I felt a warmth flood my being. The words that the others were speaking in unison came out of my mouth. And shortly Dahlia joined right in.

Chapter

21

<u>Dahlia</u>

When I got up out of Lib's bed I had no idea what awaited me. Honestly it's a good thing I didn't know. I may would've run off. The events of the day have been mind blowing. Nothing could have prepared me for what I was to bear witness to; to what I'd experience. I have been changed from the inside out. This change was drastic, unexpected and desperately needed. The gratitude I have is overwhelming.

God so loved me in spite of me to gift me with another chance to set the record, and my life, straight. The way He did it was amongst witnesses to further impress upon me the accountability necessary for change. It wasn't a bedroom revival. You know the one. Where you make promises that you will fail at keeping with tear stained pillows and a heart full of guilt. This was a full out living room camp meeting!

I'm still shocked at how things went down. I was holding on to a pain that I never should have experienced. It pushed me into areas that were detrimental to my soul. It pushed me into danger. The pain I carried for killing a man who was hurting my best friend pushed me right into the arms of his oldest daughter who wanted me dead. I was holding on to pain the way a toddler holds on to a cheese puff; relentlessly. I can't explain why I did it. It just seemed like I had to. Killing is a sinful trait that messes with you. The consequences of it are haunting you for the remainder of your days. The burden of it can sometimes be too hard to bear, so I blocked it out. Smoking, drinking, working out, and working blocked it well. Blocked it so well that it was gaining momentum to destroy me while it was being ignored. Juanita Bynum was right. "If you don't handle it, it will handle you." I heard her preach that on TV once. Man was she right. I'm living proof.

Tracy went as far as to cast spells on me. I know now why her favorite song was, "I casted a spell on you". Because the heifer really did! I don't want to say it was all her fault. I mean I have to accept responsibility; my role in all this. If I wasn't looking for love in all the wrong places, she wouldn't have ever gotten the chance to get close enough to me to put a root on me. Nigel explained everything. He was the main instrument in all of it; the uprising and the down falling. He put a spell on Tracy so that her intentions would never be detected. I see why they paid him the big bucks...I never had a clue.

He also told me why he was here today, which was to right a wrong. I can't be mad at that. There are so many things in my past I wish I had the opportunity to correct. He actually got the chance. I'm just glad he took it and didn't allow fear or people's opinions stop him. If he did, I might have been in the ground by now. He told me that the cloak has lifted and everything has been exposed. He said the threat has died down greatly. Said it's like a snake in the grass. Its ability to disguise is its protection. If its identity and location is known it becomes vulnerable. He said right now that's the condition Tracy is in.

It's not like I didn't know the day of reckoning would come. I had no idea it would be like this though. Honestly I figured Terry Dawkins would come from the grave and run me crazy. I thought that this struggle would be totally internal and not affect anyone else. I was wrong. I didn't know the man. Had no idea if he had any other children. Definitely didn't think those children would come after me, especially this hard. If I had opened my eyes to see that the love I was looking for was right in the faces of my family we wouldn't be in this mess. What I wanted, I had. That's a pattern we as humans need to break. I just knew I'd found my soul in Tracy. It wasn't in Tracy, it was in God. I ignored who He was, looking for His character in a more manipulative form, human.

Shame on me! I was led away by my own needs straight into the arms of an angry woman who was looking for a way to hurt me. I'm the one who put the welcome mat down for the devil. I let her in my life, my home, my bed, my inner circle and now my family is suffering the consequences. I still carry a sting of guilt about everyone being affected. I don't hurt people. I help people. Now I'm violent once provoked. But I'm never the instigator. To cause harm to the people that mean the most to me hurt me deeply. I'll do my very best to make it up to them, all of them. Starting with God by ditching Tracy today. Homie got to go.

So the real question is, "How will I handle Tracy?" I want to punch her smooth in the mouth right now. Don't get me wrong. I'm grateful for everything that has happened today. It has changed me in ways that are permanent. But the fight in me didn't change, at all. I'm going to do my best to just talk. I'm going to try and remain calm and have a conversation. Who am I kidding? I'm going to hit this girl. I know I am. If she comes and touches me, I'm going to knock her dead on her back and straddle her and keep punching until I feel better. That's just me. I know that I might go to jail. I've been before. Been arrested a few times behind Lib, Chevy, David, and Damian. The backseat of the cop car is an old friend. Simple assault is just that...simple. I'll deal with Tracy how I feel when she walks up on me. I won't stop God from doing His thing. I'll be obedient. But in a way I'm hoping He lets me have this one.

Adonis is here though. By him being a cop he might step in and make this an orderly interaction. And let's talk about Adonis "John the Baptist" Calloway! I've seen him around. I work at an ER and he's a cop so...yeah, I've seen him around. When I came over early this morning, thinking the worst had happened to Lib, he was here. We recognized one another and that was that. But today Adonis forged a bond with me in the come to Jesus meeting and he became my brother. I mean the way he broke everything down. After he was done talking the only thing left for me to say was either yes or no. He didn't give my mind too many opportunities to wonder and roam which sets up doubt. It was straight to the point. He's going to be a great pastor one day. Simplicity is the way. Fancy has its place but if you want to really get the grit, you've got to be blunt and honest. He was both and it was extremely effective.

I'm looking around me at the love in this living room. Everybody is acting like family. I feel like I belong. I hope they do too. The peace, laughter, and conversation going on in this room is totally separate from the living that's going on outside that door. It's an escape. I hope this is the atmosphere we provoke every single time we come together. It's so nice. Just as I was about to go get some punch from the fridge, I heard a car door slam. It got so quiet in the house. Everyone was waiting on her. I looked at David. He looked at me briefly then looked at Adonis. Adonis looked at Nigel and touched his shoulder. That's when I realized this confrontation wasn't just about me. Nigel snitched to save me. His seat is as hot as mine. And there's no way I'm going to let him face this alone. I looked at Lib. Liberty reached back and got her gun. Adonis' eyes got wide and so did his smile. I'm not sure if he was shocked or in love. That look on his face tickled me.

"Y'all?" I started. "Don't shoot the girl unless you absolutely have to. And if you have to, maim her, don't kill her. I'm not at County tonight, whoever is on staff will kill her themselves." Everybody smiled their understanding. Liberty spoke up next, "She's not allowed in my house Dee. Go out and meet that heifer on the porch. If she comes in here they'll be rolling the hearse and not the ambo." Liberty's face was stone. She had no empathy for her sister. No need to meet her. That's one thing I can say about Liberty. Once her mind is made up there is no changing it. I heard a knock and then her voice. "Dahlia?" I'm going to be honest. I wasn't sure if it was just me or not but this girl's voice has changed since our conversation earlier today. It seemed coarse and deep. Like it really didn't belong to her. I looked at David and Adonis.

Nigel winked his eye at me and he got up from the sofa. He stood behind me and said "Quti Wadarei" in just above a whisper. All of a sudden I felt a wind rushing towards us that came from absolutely nowhere. I looked back at him. His eyes were fixed above my head in some sort of trance. I looked at David and he shrugged his shoulders. I was officially scared. This thang is real! And I didn't know what to do. This is not my field of expertise. I know David dabbles in this other world. But I ain't never seen him do something like this. Somehow my brothers knew what to do. They all got up and formed a single file line that separated the sisters from the door. Man...this is some next level whodini type of carrying on!

I closed my eyes and felt Nigel's hand between my shoulder blades pushing me towards the door. I opened the door and there she stood. She didn't look like the woman I've been in love with. She looked just like her dad did all those years ago. It was like he had commandeered her body just for this moment. There were veins popping out of her neck and arms. That hasn't always been. I knew that I was going to have to really pull out all my training if I was going to fight this big demon. Let's just go ahead and call it like it is. Her calm hazel eyes had become bloodshot and wild. "Lover, are you keeping secrets from me?" She said it in a sinister way. I wanted to run honestly. But that's not my type of living. All I have to do is find a reason to get mad and I'm back to myself again. She just said I was keeping secrets. Hmm, me? That was the match to light my short fuse right there.

"Tracy," I started in a calm voice hoping to deescalate the situation before the police were called. "You are Terry Dawkins' married daughter. But I'm the one keeping secrets? Naw, you need to go ahead and leave and never come back. We're done and there's nothing for you here." I stopped talking because I knew if I kept at it, I was going to start swinging. She looked at me and said, "You killed my daddy. You didn't have to take him from me, but you did it for Liberty. Now I'm going to take you from Liberty." She lunged towards me. Liberty came out of nowhere and pushed me to the side and punched Tracy in the head twice. I looked over at Liberty while she was looking down on Tracy. Tracy was spitting out teeth and blood while she was laughing. "Hey Sis." That made Liberty's blood boil. Liberty lunged at Tracy but Adonis caught her midair and took her back in the house.

Tracy looked at me like she was ready to kill me. I walked up to her and said, "Tracy, go on now. We are good and done. Go head on." She looked at me and spit her blood on my clothes. "We're done when I say we are. You owe me Dahlia! Damn it! You fell right into my hands like a gift. I hunted you. I had to get close to you. I did many a business deals with a fool named Dade. When he'd get high his mouth would ramble. He'd tell me about his wife, Chevy and how he loved her and hated her because he could never control her. That when her friends came calling she'd run to their rescue regardless of what was going on. Then he started naming the friends one by one. Your name popped up. I knew your name from the conversations of grown folks when my daddy was killed. They say you killed him. Shot him in the head. I memorized your name. I told myself I would get you back for what you've done. So to my surprise Dade called your name. I kept asking about you. Every time we had business we'd talk about you. Whether it was guns or drugs, our meetings would always end with the topic of you. One day he said he was done talking. I couldn't have that. I was just getting to know you. I tortured him for days to get all the info I wanted. It was worth every scream. Every beg and every plea. I got off on it. Enjoyed it immensely. And that's exactly what I'm going to do to you."

She reached out to grab me. I twisted her hand off me. She pulled out a gun. I shook my head. I knew she was about to get shot. All I heard was clicking noises. Adonis started talking. "Ma'am, put your gun down." I turned around to look and there were 7 9mm pistols pointed in our direction; all four of my brothers, Liberty, Adonis and Chevy. Byrd was just pacing back and forth with her fists balled up by her sides. I'm looking around thinking that this is the end. We are all going to jail. Tracy has no chill. She's ready to die for her cause. I am not. She looked at Adonis.

"You're a cop, huh?" He said, "Yes I am. And you need to lower your weapon." That went in one ear and out of the other. She was dead set on killing me. I wasn't surrendering to her. I didn't have my hands up and they weren't going up. I will fight her back tooth and nail. Guns don't scare me. She wasn't backing down and neither was I. She had a look in her eyes that told me one of us was going to die. If it is to be, then so be it. "Ma'am, this is your last warning. Put down your weapon and get back in your vehicle and go on." Adonis' voice sounded purely professional.

There was a sound and a vibration like thunder underneath my feet. It caused me to look down and take my focus off of Tracy and her gun. The sound engulfed my senses and my nose started to bleed. There were insane vibrations. I looked back at the porch where everyone stood with their guns down looking back at Nigel. He had his hands stretched forward and his eyes were glazed over in pure white. Tracy looked up at him and called his name. "Nigel! Stop! Nigel! No!" Her voice became lost in the rumbling of the thunder. Still engulfed in a trance he said "Ab bahut ho gaya hai" over and over again. And she started screaming. She grabbed her head and screamed no over and again.

After Nigel floated down off the porch to where we were, he pushed me behind him. In the midst of the rumbling ground and her screaming he got down on one knee and put his right hand to the ground and said, "They are waiting for you Na'Treiel. Your time has come." She sat on the ground defeated. She looked at me and said "You will pay." She looked at Nigel with hopes that he could stop the ball from rolling downhill. He just looked at her. He never spoke another word. She looked at me again with malice in her eyes and evil in her smile. "I'm coming back for you lover." She quickly put the gun in her mouth, at which time I closed my eyes, and pulled the trigger. She was gone. It was only then that the rumbling stopped and the thunder ceased.

Later on that night I pulled Nigel aside to talk. He hugged me before I could begin my interrogation. The love and acceptance I felt from that one hug was enough to assure me that no matter what, everything would be alright. We stood outside on the porch while the sheriff's department investigated the untimely and unnatural death of Na'treiel James. "Nigel I have a few questions, if you don't mind." He nodded his head for me to continue. "When Tracy knocked on the door and you stood behind me, what did you say? I mean...what did it mean?" He looked off a moment and took a sip of Coke. "I said 'Quti Wadarei'. It's Arabic for 'my strength and my shield," he said. My strength and my shield. That's in Psalms. "So why was there such a gust of wind after you said it?" He smiled at me. I know my eyebrows are tangled in confusion. But I've just got to know.

"Dahlia the wind represented the movement of angels getting into place to be just what I asked for, strength and a shield." I'm nodding my head in understanding but the puzzle still needs to be solved. "Okay so what were you looking at after you said it? It was like you weren't with us. What did you see?" He took another sip of coke and looked at me with a twinkle in his eyes. "I saw the fight in a different realm. I have to use what I've got to do the good that I'm supposed to. I can't fight in the natural. Not that I don't have the skill. But if you fist fight only you don't really end the fight. You've got to deal with the spiritual wickedness in high places. If not you'll continue the fight with the same devil in a different body. Liberty fought the body, I dealt with the soul."

That's a mouth full right there! I never thought about it that way. "So the whole time your eyes were glazed over, you were warring in the spirit?" He just nodded his head. I'm starting to get it. This magick thing is starting to make sense. "Okay, two more questions." He laughed at me. I laughed with him. "What was the last thing you said before you floated off the porch?" He looked at me with confusion on his face. "I floated off the porch? Me? Naw I don't remember that." I just nodded my head like a stubborn kid who was promised ice cream by a busy dad trying to get out of going to the store. "Ab bahut ho gaya hai' means enough is enough in Hindi. It was time to end the fight before things got out of hand. Let me guess, the other question was about the thunder in the ground?" I just nodded my head.

"Tracy made some deals with some very powerful demons, her father being one of them. They had made good on their end of the bargain. But she didn't deliver. The contract was reneged and they wanted their pay which ended up being her soul. They wanted you dead Dahlia. She couldn't deliver. It took too long and the spirits became impatient." I began to cry. This was messed up! I had a contract on me from hell. Now you hear preachers say things like that all the time. But to hear it like this? It shook me to my core. I had to sit down. He came and sat down right beside me.

"Dahlia, you've got some decisions to make, and soon. I'm not one to tell you how to live your life or who to love. But it's time to do what you need to do. It's not the time to see just how far you can push a boundary. It is evident that you are wanted by both entities, hell and heaven. You need to choose one before one is chosen for you. You're not going to be able to live long with hell after you this hard. Your protection will run out eventually if you don't choose who's protecting you. And you'll have to choose daily until it becomes less of a struggle. It's going to be alright, even if it doesn't feel like it's alright right now. I'm going to tell you what was told to me when I was at this kind of crossroads in my life. The preacher told me the devil was going to try and kill me because he didn't want to lose me. But if I really wanted to change for the better, I'd fight for my life. He looked me in the eye and told me 'If you live through the next two months of hell, you will be able to make it through anything'. That was thirteen months ago. If I can make it, you can too. Dahlia, fight for your life."

He put his arm around me and we sat in silence until the officers were finished with their investigation and were cleaning up. I decided to do right by me and fight for my life. I deserve peace and joy. I deserve to be happy and feel loved whether I'm in a relationship or not. That comes from within. I want this. And I will do whatever it takes to have it. Including leaving women alone. I have said it before, if ever God calls for me I will answer and leave my kind of love behind.

One Year Later

<u>Chevy</u>

"**D**ahlia?! Get off me with your big and heavy behind!" Dahlia looked at me like I'd hurt her feelings. I burst out laughing. I know good and dog-gone well she's gained at least 15 pounds in the last year or so. I mean it is a healthy weight, but it's still weight and weight is heavy. "I'm just so happy to see you, Chevy. I'm so excited about this girl's vacay that I don't know what to do!" "Dee it's good to see you too. I know I just saw you last weekend but this feels different. I'm going to be honest with you. It feels almost exotic. Now I know our bonds as sisters have strengthened, however it does not require you to get in my lap when we're together." Dahlia laughed and said, "But I used to sit in your lap all the time when we were in high school." I gave her the side eye and told her the haggard truth, "I was a lot stronger then and you were a lot smaller. Those days have come and they have gone." She patted me on the back like she felt sorry for me. I swatted at her hand. She giggled and pinched my thigh. This girl is always meddling! At least she's happy. Dahlia has changed dramatically. The cares and troubles of her existence no longer bothers her. She's happy, healthy, single, saved and stress free. I've never seen her this way before. But I love it!

We've gotten together for our first annual girls celebration. Today marks exactly one year of big changes, coming together as family, spilling of secrets and the death of Tracy. Oh it was a big to do! We were all interviewed, detained, and released. The whole Columbia had a field day over "The Suicide Death of a New Orleans Native". Adonis handled everything and we didn't have to be in the eye of the storm or the public very long.

Truth be told, I was worried about Dahlia. It would've bothered me if I saw the person that I was ready to commit my heart and life to just 24 hours earlier kill herself. But boy did she surprise me! She took a leave of absence from work, which was a shocker because it was allergy season and Dee's a workaholic. Plus she went and signed up for counseling the next day. She's had her moments as we all did, but for the most part she's doing very well. She apologized to me. It hurt her that her decision to help Liberty all those years ago ended up getting my husband killed and in such a brutal way.

Let's face it; Nathan Devonte' "Dade" Davidson needed to die. There was no good in him. It took a lot of soul searching for me to come to that conclusion. But it was the truth. Deep down I knew it all along. He was the devil's advocate in some situations and just the pure devil in others. I think it's only fair that he was killed because of someone else with as many people as he has hurt. I know he's done some awful things. I know for myself that he was guilty of solicitation of murder on several counts. I told Dahlia that I've made peace with the whole situation because I didn't want her to carry around a guilt that didn't belong to her. Also because I didn't want her to know that I couldn't care less about Dade and that would make me sound so heartless and cold. Good news is I'm free of him now.

The only reminder of him that I have is young Sir Adrian. He's such a sweetheart. He, his mother, and I, have gotten extremely close. He calls me Aunt Chevy. He comes to spend every weekend with me and his mother comes to eat Sunday dinner with us. I tell him whatever he wants to know about his dad. The money, the drugs, the laughter, the sports; everything.

Speaking of free. God has done wondrous things for me, my attitude and my habits. I've been sober for over a year now. I haven't been bed hopping either. My "ho cake" days are behind me. Evan and I have gotten serious with one another. He even asked me to marry him. I said yes of course. I couldn't deny those big sad brown eyes. We're set to tie the knot in 4 months. I'm ridiculously excited! I didn't get a wedding the first time around. I got a preacher and a witness in the pastor's office on a Wednesday night before bible study. I know, such a romance! But in four months? I'm going to be a bride with bridesmaids and cake; lots of cake. And I can't wait.

Byrd just got engaged too. Her wedding is after her last semester is over. You gotta know Byrd. Her priorities are on point and in a straight line. Nothing and no one will stop her from her goal. Nigel is so good for her. He's become a brother to all of us. When there is a gathering, which is once a month, he's right there cooking between the Emerley Men. He's taught us a lot on how to deal with situations, emotions, and past experiences. He and Adonis have become like our own personal counselors.

Adonis is now pastoring...big surprise right? He has one of the larger churches in the county in the middle of nowhere. It's a nice, clean and simple establishment amongst many trees. He named it Freedom Chapel Non-Denominational Church. I attend every Sunday, Wednesday and Saturday night. I don't teach, or sing. I do talk though, in bible study. Adonis also has me on the board of advisement. He said I was an invaluable asset and that I could be counted on to just tell it like it is. And sometimes "Brother Pastor" will call me up to help him pray for someone. I never thought I'd be a participating member of anyone's church. Not me, the drunken one!

"Well well well...look who is here and on time. Byrd, you were flying weren't you?" Byrd looked so innocent when she said, "Me? Never!" We all fell out laughing because we all know that she has a very heavy foot. "What's going on Chevrolet?" I pinched her behind and she squealed. I hate it when she calls me that. She's the only one who does. Probably because I've put fear in everybody else who has tried it. "Now Byrd, go fly right over there by Dahlia. Maybe the two of you can meddle with each other until the both of you are satisfied." I sounded just like my mama when I said that. I am scheduled to go away with her next weekend. She wants to go to Mobile Alabama to the flea market on Schillingers. She called me up and told me she had some extra money and she was ready to "shop". That is at least four and a half hours in the hot sun wandering from booth to booth. But whatever makes her happy.

In walks Lib. She is so prissy lately. She has changed dramatically. Her demeanor is much more pleasant than it used to be. Probably because she's a first lady now. Yes ma'am and yes sir! Liberty and Adonis got married four months after meeting. He makes her happy. Most importantly he makes her humble! Liberty is a joy to be around now. She's full of life, laughter and fun. We all talk every day. Liberty has been instrumental in all of our walks of getting it together. "Hello heifers!" She squealed. "I'm so excited to be here! This hotel is absolutely beautiful. I wonder if they've got cheesecake on the room service menu?" We all fell out laughing. Liberty is a cheesecake fanatic! No matter what, she's going to have a piece of cheesecake and it doesn't matter the flavor or what mood she's in. I've seen the girl crying, I mean an ugly cry, and shoveling turtle cheesecake in her face at the same time.

While we are on this well-deserved trip, the men in our lives are on one too. They decided to bond as brothers while we show out as sisters. All four of Marjorie Santana Emerley's sons, Evan, Adonis, and Nigel are on a two day fishing trip. I've already gotten pictures of the three fish that were caught. They will definitely be eating cereal tonight. I don't think all three of those fish are big enough to be a sandwich for just one of them. I told Evan to chew some tobacco and spit it on the bait. It works like magic. He scrunched up his face and asked me how I even knew that. I laughed at him and said "You should've met my Daddy. He was a fisherman from the depths of his heart." He shook his head and walked away. But he did text me to say that David had a can of the "chew" with him. I hollered!

"May I have your attention please?" Liberty has started the toasting process. She's always taking over. We normally just let her, with her bossy self. "I just want to say how proud I am of all of us. We've come so far in the last twelve months. Our love for each other has been clearly shown and not just told. We've grown up to be lovely young ladies with joy and peace. We've all been given second chances. And I couldn't be more grateful. This year alone has been proof that when you die you are stuck with no do overs. But when the blood runs warm in your veins you still have time to make things right. It's never too late to change. It's never too late to love. Now, I have a little gift for all of you. But I want you to all open them at the same time." She gets up and starts passing out these cute boxes wrapped in white with our name written in script in silver. "Okay open them in one, two, three!" In the box was black tissue paper and a mug that read "Promoted From Bestie to Auntie". In the mug was a sonogram of the cutest little bean I've ever seen! We all started squealing and crying. The excitement was overwhelming and we all surrounded Liberty with hugs, kisses, and wet faces. Our lives have started fresh. Our family has and will continue to enlarge. Our love has strengthened. And our souls now rejoice.

The End

About the Author

Sugar, Shalonda Rawls, is a small business owner that lives in Columbia Mississippi. Reading was instilled in her from the womb and so was creative expression. Learning and participating in everything from jewelry making to poetry, creativity has always been a part of her being. She has fallen in love with what she calls "conversational ministry" and is currently working on the next novel. Some of the authors that have inspired her throughout the years are Bernice McFadden, Francine Rivers, Lutisha Lovely, and Peron Long. She states that she would love to be named among the greats but is extremely grateful to be heard more than anything. Be on the lookout for more content. She'd love to hear from you!

Email her at sugarof85@gmail.com Give it about 2-3 business days but you'll surely get a reply.